The Trail Journey of J.D. and the Princess

Rita Floriani

The thru-hikers and all trail names depicted in this story were inspired by the one thousand and one actual Appalachian Trail thru-hikers the author has met over the years. Any resemblance to any actual thru-hiker or trail name or any off trail person is purely coincidental. Although the author has attempted to portray as accurately as possible the Appalachian Trail in Pennsylvania in this fictional account, please consult actual Appalachian Trail guidebooks for complete and current trail information. Strictly fictional places in this work are the "Hiker Bistro and Bar" in Duncannon, the "Little Bear Pub" in Port Clinton and the "Hiker Hostel Gazebo in the Park" in Port Clinton. All water in the wilderness should always be treated and proper footwear and hiking gear should always be used.

The author, a lifelong resident of the state of Pennsylvania, hikes often on the Appalachian Trail.

All photos on the covers and in the text are by Rita Floriani.

Front cover photo: The Appalachian Trail, PA Route 501 trailhead.

Back cover photo: View from the Pinnacle, 80 yards from the Appalachian Trail in Pennsylvania, looking northeast to the Blue Mountain, on which runs the Appalachian Trail.

Released 2015 with trail updates

ISBN-10: 1497414490
ISBN-13: 978-1497414495

Dedication

To all hikers on the trail of life,
who share their humor, enthusiasm and
encouragement with their companions
and to all who have ever raised their eyes to
the mountains for help.

The Appalachian Trail sign on PA Route 183.

Chapter 1

It might have been close to three in the afternoon when Collin Talley opened his eyes, but it didn't matter to him what time it was, nor did he care that he had slept the day away.

Lying on his back with his arms folded beneath his head, in a bed of prairie grass and warmed by the early spring sun, he stared up into the bluest sky he had ever seen.

He was at his secret place near the billboard on the interstate, missing yet another day of school. It wasn't his original plan to skip school that day. He had really intended on going. His books were in his hands, but just as he was putting them into his backpack, he heard the weather report from the television in the family room.

"If you were thinking of taking a vacation day, this is the day to do it," the meteorologist had said. "There will be nothing but sunshine and blue skies and the temperature is expected to hit seventy. That's right folks, seventy degrees. That's a record high for a day so early in spring. Get out and enjoy it while you can, because even though we have all this gorgeous sunshine today, we do expect the temperature to drop and clouds to roll into our area late tonight."

"Get out and enjoy it" were the only words Collin needed to hear and he knew he would not be spending one second of the day inside. The winter had been too long and cold. How could he be sitting in school when this day was so incredibly warm and full of sunshine?

So what if he skipped another day? He didn't care how many days he had already missed. Besides, what were they going to do to him anyway? Yell at him? Lecture him? Make him do community service?

His foster family the Meckleys couldn't get him to do simple chores around the farm. His county caseworker was too swamped with kids in Lincoln to come all the way out to Kepner Creek. The principal in school had already told him he was not worth the effort of his time and the school guidance counselor was useless, so Collin knew he was home free to do what he wanted.

The horn of a tractor-trailer blew loudly from the other side of the long split-rail fence and Collin got up, climbed up the side of the billboard and stared at the traffic on the highway from his bird's eye view. He watched as a small sports car cut into the right lane just in front of the truck in order to pass a slower moving car that was driving unhurriedly in the passing lane. As soon as the small sports car drove past the slow moving car, it cut back into the passing lane and took off, disappearing into the horizon.

Collin climbed off the billboard and went over to the fence. Not a cop in sight, he thought as he looked in both directions of the interstate. Nothing but cars and trucks in a continuous caravan of people heading east and west over the unending Nebraska prairie. Day or night, weekday or weekend, people were always going somewhere. Where were they going, he wondered. Where were they coming from?

He wondered what it would be like to have some place to go, to be free to just hop in a car, jump on the highway and take off to somewhere far away.

Somewhere where something was happening and there were things to do and places to see, places far from these dull flat fields of nothing.

Turning away from his secret place by the side of the road, Collin cut through fields and reached the narrow road that led back to the small town of Kepner Creek. There was no steady stream of cars on this back road. In fact, there were no cars at all.

He was totally alone until he turned at the junction and saw the patrol car sitting by the side of the road.

"Get in, Talley," the deputy called to him, motioning to the front seat. "Don't make me chase you."

"No, thanks. I can walk from here," Collin said to him, considering momentarily making the deputy get out of his car to stop him.

"Get in the car," the deputy called to him again.

Collin yawned. He was hungry and he didn't feel like running.

"Where were you?" the deputy asked him as Collin got in the car and pulled the door closed.

"Nowhere. It's Kepner Creek and that's about as nowhere as you can get."

"You weren't in Kepner Creek. I was looking for you all day in town and you were nowhere in sight. You missed a whole day of school again. The judge isn't going to like this at all. Why can't you try to follow the rules? I mean it, Talley. All you have to do is try a little. It's not a hard thing to do."

"Where are we going?" Collin asked when the deputy turned toward town, the opposite direction of where he was staying. "Aren't you going to drop me off at the farm?"

"This isn't a taxi cab, Talley. When you didn't show up for school, your caseworker had no alternative but to call me. You were walking a thin line as it was. We're going to the courthouse where the judge is waiting to see you."

"Let him wait," said Collin in his cocky tone, "because I have nothing to say to him."

"Well, he has plenty to say to you."

The deputy pulled up in front of the small town's courthouse and escorted him inside to an empty courtroom.

"Wait here," said the deputy. "If you're not here when I get back, I promise you a ride immediately to the State Juvenile Detention Center. Do you hear me?"

"Whatever. Don't make such a big thing out of it."

The deputy shook his head and left Collin to wait in a courtroom by himself. As the minutes passed by, Collin put his feet up on the long bench and made himself comfortable. Just a short time ago, he was staring up at the deep blue endless sky; now he was stuck inside, staring up at an ugly beige ceiling.

Nearly twenty minutes passed by until he heard footsteps approaching and the door opened.

Collin watched as Mrs. Kintner, his caseworker, and Mr. Meckley, his foster father, entered the room.

"Collin," Mr. Meckley whispered to him. "Where were you? Why weren't you in school today?"

"Why does everybody have to make such a big deal of this?" Collin asked. "I skip school one day and I'm like number one on the FBI's most wanted list."

"It's been a lot more than just one day, Mr. Talley," said Mrs. Kintner. "You said you weren't going to do this any more."

The deputy returned.

"Everyone rise," he said.

The judge entered the room and sat down. Opening a file, he paged through it. Finally he pointed to Collin.

"Young man, approach the bench."

Collin walked up to the judge.

"Why weren't you in school today?" the judge asked him.

Collin shrugged.

"I asked you a question," the judge said, his voice growing louder. "And I want an answer."

"Because I didn't want to go. I hate that school and I hate this town."

"Fine. I'm sure you will like the confines of the State Juvenile Detention Center much more than our little town. They have barbed-wire fences. They have locked doors. They have a lot more structure and rules than you have here. Deputy, you may take him there right now."

As the deputy placed handcuffs on Collin's wrists, the door to the courtroom opened and a man walked in.

"Your honor, please. Can I have one moment?"

"Curtis Everett," said the judge, recognizing the man. "You may approach the bench."

The judge motioned for the deputy to wait and then nodded to Everett.

"Your honor," he began, looking at both the judge and the caseworker. "I have only been this young man's English teacher since January. I know Collin Talley has not been cooperative." He looked over at Mr. Meckley. "I know he does not do his chores on the farm." Then he looked at Collin. "I know first-hand that he has done very poorly on his tests and that he doesn't turn in his homework assignments. And I know he's missed countless days of school." Then he looked back up at the judge. "But, there has to be a better alternative than sending him to a state facility. Collin is not a bad kid. He doesn't do drugs. He doesn't steal. He's not rowdy. He doesn't get into fights unless someone else starts them, and then I don't blame him for defending himself, especially when he is outnumbered, which is usually how it is. Please, your honor, for his sake we need to give him one more chance. I will work with him on his schoolwork, but please don't put him in jail."

For a moment everyone was silent, waiting to see what the judge would say.

"Mrs. Kintner," the judge began. "What do you have to say about this?"

"It is obvious that the Meckleys have tried. However, Collin has not. As Mr. Everett has plainly stated, Collin's behavior is poor at best. He does not do simple chores at the Meckleys. He does not do his schoolwork. And as far as Collin's attendance in school, for every one day he is there, he skips two. I recommend that he be adjudicated delinquent and be placed in a stricter environment."

"Mr. Meckley," the judge said to Collin's foster parent. "Do you have anything to say about this young man?"

"Yes, your honor. Collin is the first foster child my wife and I have taken in. I'm asking you to give us one more chance with him. He's had almost fifteen years working at what he is. He can't change into something else overnight. No one can. It must be difficult for him, living on a farm and being a part of a family he doesn't know. But my children like him and I feel if he is given more time, I know things will improve. Give us another chance, then if things don't work out..." He stopped. He did not want to say Collin should go to the juvenile facility, but it was plain that was where Collin would go if he blew this last chance.

"Collin Talley," the judge said in his loudest and sternest voice. "You have been truant from school for the last time today. If it wasn't for your teacher here, and Mr. Meckley, you would be on your way to the state juvenile lockup. When you leave here, you will go back to the farm and do whatever chores the Meckleys ask you to do. Tomorrow you will go to school and you will do your schoolwork. This is your very last chance. Do you hear me?"

"Yeah," said Collin. "Whatever."

"No!" the judge yelled. "It's not whatever. It's your last chance. Don't blow it!"

The judge rose and left the courtroom.

"You're lucky," the deputy said to Collin, removing the cuffs. "You better do what he says or I'll be seeing you again real soon."

"C'mon," Mr. Meckley said to Collin. "Let's go home."

But Collin's teacher stopped them.

"Can you give me a moment with the boy?"

Meckley nodded. "I'll be at the truck, Collin."

Curtis Everett stood with Collin in the empty courtroom.

"Collin," the teacher began. "Everybody has to do stuff they don't like to do. But you're the first person I met that doesn't want to do anything at all. You don't do homework. You don't take part in any sports or activities. You don't do anything to help out at the Meckleys. Isn't there anything you like to do? Anything at all? Ride a bike? Draw pictures?"

"I guess," Collin started. "I guess I just like to be left alone."

"Yeah, I feel like that sometimes, too. But not all the time." He pulled a paperback book from his coat pocket. "You missed a great speaker at assembly today, but everything he said is in his book. I want you to take it and read it. You don't even have to write a report on it. But I want to discuss it with you and I want to know what you think about it. Okay?"

Collin looked at the title, *Walking the High Mountain Ridge*.

"I don't know," said Collin. "What do I know about mountains? There are no mountains around for a thousand miles."

"Just read it," the teacher said to him. "You might not think you can relate to it, but the story is about a guy just a couple years older than you and he was from farm country, too. Look, Collin, we all got our own mountains to climb. Take the book, start reading it tonight. Read a little bit each night. You'll like it. I know you will."

His teacher pointed to the title page.

"And look, he even autographed it," he said, smiling proudly like the signature itself was a special treasure.

"But I got chores to do," Collin said, trying his best to get out of the assignment, even as easy as his teacher was trying to make it for him.

"I'm not asking you to read the whole thing in one night. Try one page. If you can't read one page a night, then try for one paragraph. That's all. Just try it. Okay?"

Collin shrugged and took the book and headed outside to the pickup truck parked at the curb.

"I know you are not happy. I'm sorry about that," Mr. Meckley said to Collin as he hopped in the truck. "If there was something I could do…"

Collin stared out the window, avoiding his guardian's attempts to talk to him.

"I don't treat you any better or worse than any of my own kids. I never have. I don't even think of you as not being one of my own."

They drove on in silence. When they reached the driveway that led to the farmhouse, Meckley spoke again.

"Your birthday is in two weeks. Is there anything really special you'd like?"

"Yeah, a car," said Collin.

"You're only going to be fifteen."

"That's the only thing I want."

"Maybe next year. Of course, it wouldn't be a brand new car or too expensive, and you'd have to get a job to pay for the insurance."

Yeah, right, like this guy was going to buy a car for a foster kid, Collin thought to himself. It didn't matter anyway even if Adam Meckley spoke the truth; Collin knew that there was no way he was going to be around here that long. One day soon he knew he was going to leave, head out to the highway, stick out his thumb and get in the first car that pulled over to give him a lift.

"Collin," Mr. Meckley said, as they got out of the truck and stood at the back of the house. "We're going to expand the garden area here."

He led the boy to the tool shed and showed him the small tractor.

"The earth must be tilled. Sit yourself down and I'll show you how to operate this equipment."

"But I'm hungry," said Collin.

“Dinner will be ready in half an hour. You’ll be amazed at how much you can get done in that time.”

He gave Collin a few simple instructions.

“But, I have a lot of homework,” said Collin, stalling from doing the job at hand. “I have to read this book for school.”

“Son, believe it or not, I have every confidence that you can do both the tilling and read your book. Go on now and get started.”

Collin took off for the north end of the yard, to what would be the farthest section of the garden. As he disappeared behind a row of young apple trees, he turned off the motor and pulled out the book from the pocket of his hoodie.

“*Walking the High Mountain Ridge* by Wyatt ‘Far to Go’ Thornton,” he read aloud. He fanned through the pages and it opened to the inside cover where his teacher’s name and address were on an embossed decorative label.

“I don’t want to read your stupid book,” he said, raising the book to hurl it onto the compost pile that Mrs. Meckley had started. For a moment he hesitated as the words that the teacher had said that day in the courtroom came back to him.

“Collin is not a bad kid.”

“Yeah, maybe I am,” said Collin.

He tossed the book onto the ground, turned on the tractor and rode it in no set pattern or direction until he knew it was time to eat and went into the house.

He ate supper as he always did, in silence. He never had anything to say, but even if he did, he didn’t have much of a chance to say it with Adam and Kate Meckley’s kids at the table. Six year old Jory, eight year old Josh and nine year old Kaitlyn talked nonstop through each mealtime.

Why the county children's service sent him here to be with this family, Collin didn't know. He was used to surviving on the streets, in shelters, in group homes, and the county juvenile detention centers he had to stay at when he was picked up for his persistent truancy and his constant running away.

What did he know about living with a nice family like this and their perfectly nice house and their perfect kids who enjoyed doing their chores and hanging out with their little friends? What did he know about farming?

So maybe they were okay and nice to him, but this lifestyle was so different from anything he knew. Sometimes he would stare at Jory, the youngest boy and wonder what it must be like to be him, to grow up having both parents always there and to have his own bed and his own room and be safe and protected from life out on the streets. He watched how Jory and Josh dressed like their dad, even wearing the same kind of hat, and how they helped him on the farm. He watched how Kaitlyn helped her mom in the kitchen and how she sometimes cooked the meals all by herself. The little girl took care of the chickens, looked out for all the kittens that roamed the farm and was preparing the garden for the new planting season.

When he first arrived at their place at the beginning of the year, Collin thought it was so Mr. Meckley would have free labor to help on the farm. Collin didn't like that. When he was given some chores, Collin put off doing them for so long that after a while, they no longer asked him to help out. He thought for sure they would have sent him away, but they didn't.

Alone in his thoughts, Collin felt that any normal person would have been happy to have a warm, comfortable place to stay and good meals. That should have been enough for him, but it wasn't.

He didn't like the school that they sent him to in town. Nobody there was open to having an outsider join them, especially when they heard he was a foster kid. The kids in his class had been together since kindergarten and no new kid had ever showed up like that in the middle of the year. They didn't know what to think of him. He wasn't outgoing, but he didn't appear to be timid. He did not talk but it wasn't because they thought he was shy. At first some of the girls wanted to know where he was from and tried to talk to him, but Collin never shared anything about himself and he didn't express any interest in anyone at the school. The guys watched him warily and saw him as competition for their girlfriends and tried, mostly unsuccessfully, to provoke him into fighting.

There were all kinds of rumors going through the school about him from the moment he got there, false rumors of a troubled past, false rumors of a juvenile record that seemed to grow longer and more violent as the weeks went by. There was no real effort to make him feel welcome, but he never tried to fit in either so he kept to himself as much as he could.

Collin didn't want to be there, not at that school, not at that farm, not in that small quiet country town called Kepner Creek.

As soon as he finished eating, Collin went up to his room. He lay down on his bed with his headphones, killing time until it was too dark to go back outside and finish the tilling.

He heard the phone ringing around nine and was surprised when Mrs. Meckley knocked on his door and said the call was for him.

"For me?" Collin wondered who it could be. No one ever called him.

Chapter 2

He took the phone from his foster mom.

"Yeah?" he said.

"So how do you like his trail name?"

"What?" Collin asked. "What are you talking about? Who is this?"

"It's Curtis Everett, your English teacher. So what do you think of Wyatt's trail name?"

"I don't know what you're talking about."

"Oh, I see you didn't start the book yet," said the teacher. "See, the author talks all about his trail name in the first couple pages. I'm surprised you haven't finished the first few chapters already. It's fast reading."

"I had chores to do," said Collin.

"Well, I hope you get to read at least the first chapter. If not, like I said, read a paragraph. I'll see you tomorrow and we'll talk about it."

"Yeah, whatever."

Collin ended the call and returned the phone to his foster mom. He was probably the only kid at school who didn't text, instant message, or twitter, the only kid who didn't have his own smartphone or iPad. But who was there to text? Who was there to talk to? No one.

Outside the wind picked up even before he fell asleep and it grew stronger as the night wore on. The temperature dropped and the rain began to fall.

The house was quiet, except for the howling wind outside. Collin's sleep was interrupted by the same dream he had almost every night since he came there to live. He was standing by the highway watching the cars.

"Hey, where are you going?" he called to them. "Where are you going?"

No one would ever answer him. No one would ever stop.

Sometimes the cars would slow down and they would stare at him as they cruised by. Once a pickup truck came by. Surely he would be fast enough to jump in the back, but no matter how fast Collin ran, the pickup was always just inches out of reach.

"Stop," he yelled. "Please stop and give me a ride. Please take me with you."

But the never ending line of cars just kept going.

Then he heard something. Something from far away. Voices were crying out to him.

"We have far to go," they said.

"I want to have far to go, too," he called to the cars, trying to get them to stop.

But they did not stop. They sped by, leaving him standing alone. Yet he could still hear them calling to him.

"We have far to go… we have far to go…"

Unlike his past dreams where he simply stood by the side of the road with his thumb out, tonight he knew he had to do something different. He stepped out onto the highway determined to get someone's attention. He was going to make someone stop no matter what.

He turned to face the oncoming cars. One car came heading straight towards him. Surely it would stop. The lights were so bright and blinding. But it did not slow down. It just kept coming. There was no way he could get out of the way, so he threw up his arm.

A crash, so horrifically loud, awoke Collin with such a start from his dream that he bolted up out of bed.

"What was that?" he called out drenched in sweat. He looked at the clock. It was after midnight. Thunder was roaring from the storm outside and lightning flashed across the sky. Collin looked out the window at the rain pouring down in fierce blinding torrents.

For a while he stood silently watching the rain covering the earth and furiously hitting the window at a slant.

And then he thought about the book he had tossed to the ground.

"Collin is not a bad kid," his teacher's words came back to him.

"Yeah," said Collin. "I am."

He left the window and sat on the edge of his bed.

"Collin is not a bad kid," he heard the teacher's words again.

He could tell the teacher liked the book. He could tell the teacher liked it that the guy who wrote it came and gave a talk at their school. Then Everett brought that book all the way over to the courthouse to give it to him. But Collin knew the book wasn't the reason the teacher showed up there. He went to speak up for Collin so the judge would cut him a break and give him another chance.

"Darn you, Everett," Collin said, standing up. "Why did you have to be nice?"

By now, that book had to be ruined, Collin thought. It had to be soaked in the drenching rain and mud. Maybe there was still a chance that he could retrieve the book and dry it out without too much damage.

He ran downstairs and out the backdoor, barefoot and wearing nothing but a cut-off pair of gray sweatpants. Though it would only take a second to get it, he was halfway across the barely tilled garden patch when he regretted not having thrown on a shirt and jacket and not having grabbed an umbrella or a flashlight.

He reached the area where he had tossed the book, but he didn't see it, even when the lightning lit up the sky.

"Where is it?" he asked aloud.

He walked up and down the yard, but he couldn't find it anywhere.

Ten, fifteen, twenty minutes passed by. It was freezing cold, nothing at all like the warm, sun-filled day before.

He returned to the compost pile. On his hands and knees he pushed through the mud with his fingers. Shivering and soaked through and through, he was not going to quit until he found it.

Maybe the wind had picked it up and blew it further away, he thought to himself. He stood up and walked around in a larger and larger circle.

No, he thought. It had to be where he tossed it and he went back to clawing at the mud. This had to be the place where he had thrown it. Why couldn't he find it? It couldn't have just disappeared.

The water ran down his face, blinding him, but he had nothing but the back of his mud covered hands to push the water out of his eyes.

More and more time was passing by, but he kept trying.

Had he tilled it under with the tractor?

He searched deeper into the mud with his hands. It didn't make sense that he couldn't find it. Finally after more than an hour, he felt defeated and his shoulders sank in hopeless resignation.

"Stupid book," he mumbled as one warm drop ran down his cold face. "Stupid teacher."

He turned to go back to the house and slipped, falling face first in the mud. He tried to get up, fell again, and crawled until he reached a section of fence then pulled himself up and stumbled back to the house.

He turned the doorknob, but the wind blew open the door and slammed it inside forcefully against the kitchen wall. He didn't know what exploded louder, the howling storm or Kaitlyn's scream as he stepped inside.

Why was she screaming like that, he wondered.

In an instant, Adam and Kate Meckley were in the kitchen. Fear and anger showed on their faces. In Adam's hand was an axe. Kate grabbed Kaitlyn and held her tight. It took them one long moment to realize that it wasn't a filthy, homicidal maniac who had broken into their home and was standing there in the doorway.

"Collin?" Mr. Meckley asked calmly, as he slowly put the axe on the counter. "What are you doing? What were you doing outside?"

Collin couldn't make his teeth stop chattering long enough to answer him.

Kate saw a larger and larger puddle of water and mud forming on the floor where Collin stood.

"It's okay, baby," Kate said putting her daughter down. "It's okay. It's Collin. Go on and get the afghan off the sofa."

Kaitlyn left the kitchen and Adam went over and closed the kitchen door.

"Collin," he said, taking the boy's arm. "What is going on? Why were you outside?"

"I had to look for the book," said Collin.

Adam looked over at his wife.

"Is he sleep walking?" she asked Adam.

Adam shook his head and shrugged.

"I couldn't find it," Collin said to them.

Never in all his years on the farm did Adam ever remember a day when he was as filthy and covered with dirt as Collin was now.

"You should take him upstairs," Kate spoke up.

"Not like this."

Kaitlyn returned with the afghan and handed it to her mom.

"Adam, he's about to freeze to death. Put this around him."

"Hold it a second," he said to her. "Come here, Collin."

He led Collin over to the mud room beside the kitchen. He filled a bucket at the large sink with warm water. Using a towel he removed as much mud from Collin's face, hands and feet as he could. He then took the bucket of warm water and poured it over the boy.

Collin's gray cutoffs, now black from the mud, dripped muddy water down his legs and onto the floor. Adam took the afghan from his wife and wrapped it around Collin then helped him upstairs.

"Get in and take a hot shower, Collin," said Adam. "I'll get you some dry clothes."

Dressed in warm fleece clothes and wrapped in an electric blanket set on high, Collin began to thaw out.

"People die from hypothermia," Adam said to Collin gently. "I don't know what was so important, but don't you ever go out again in cold, rainy weather dressed like you were!"

Collin nodded.

"Are you feeling warmer?" he continued.

Again Collin nodded.

Kate brought a cup of hot chocolate for him, but when she tried handing the cup to him, his fingers were still shaking.

"I'm not thirsty. I just want to sleep."

"I'll hold it for you," she said. "But you have to take a sip or two."

"No, I'm tired," he said, burying the side of his face into his pillow and closing his eyes.

"Okay, then," said Kate, "I'll turn off the overhead light, but I'm going to leave the desk lamp on. If you need anything, let us know, okay?"

He responded with just the slightest nod and fell asleep.

"I'm going to check on Kaitlyn," she said to her husband. "Do you think he'll be all right?"

"I don't know," Adam told her. "I think I'll sit here a little while and keep an eye on him."

Chapter 3

Wrapped tightly in warm blankets, Collin slept peacefully, dreaming he was in a quiet flower-filled meadow under a very hot sun on a cloudless day. The heat did not bother him and he wanted to stay right where he was. But there was a sound or a rustling coming from somewhere. Where? He did not know, but it made him stir.

He opened his eyes and for a moment he did not know where he was. He saw daylight streaming in the window like it was late morning.

Sensing someone was near, he looked up and saw the deputy was standing in the doorway of his bedroom.

"What are you doing here?" Collin whispered, wondering if he was in the middle of a nightmare. Then Collin's eyes fell to the clock on his desk. "Ten thirty? No. That can't be right!" He groaned and tried to sit up, but he didn't have the energy. Nor could he bring himself to abandon his blankets for he did not feel warm enough to emerge from them into the cold of his room. "I overslept, but I don't know why… I set the alarm…I don't want to be late for school."

"Take it easy, kid," the deputy said, coming over and touching his forehead. "The day when you are worried that you're going to be late for school is the day when I know for sure that you're sick. Rest easy, kid. You don't have to go anywhere today."

"Just give me a minute. I'll get ready, but why is it so cold in here?" Collin whispered, before falling back asleep.

The deputy shook his head. The room was so warm that he had to take off his jacket.

"I'm really sorry I didn't call the school," said Kate, who Collin didn't see was standing on the other side of his room. "It was a little busy here, between Collin and Kaitlyn."

"No worries," said the deputy. "What's wrong with Kaitlyn?"

"She didn't feel well this morning, so I kept her home. I don't think she slept all night." Kate reached down and touched Collin's face. "He has a fever. He probably has pneumonia. We should have taken him to the hospital last night."

"Kids are resilient, especially that one there. Unless he has trouble breathing, I'm sure he'll be fine. What was he doing out there last night?"

"He said something about looking for a book. I don't know. Maybe he was hallucinating."

Mrs. Meckley looked in the doorway and saw Kaitlyn standing there.

"How are you doing there, Kaitlyn?"

"Mommy, I know what book he's talking about. I found it last night when I went out to the compost pile. I didn't know why it was there."

"What did you do with it?" her mom asked her.

"I left it in the shed with the wheelbarrow."

"Well, he'll be happy to hear that," she said.

"Looks like he does care about something," said the deputy. "I better get going. I'll see myself out."

Kaitlyn went out to the shed and brought the book up to Collin's room. At first she stood there and wondered where she should put it then decided she should wake up Collin and ask him.

Climbing up on his bed she touched his hands where he clutched the blanket up at his chest.

"Collin," she whispered, shaking his hands. "I have your book and it's okay."

He opened his eyes.

"What?" he whispered.

"Your book is okay. Not even a drop of rain or a piece of mud touched it."

He looked at her and then at the book in her hands. Reaching for it, he took it and stared at it.

Where did she find it, he wondered.

She touched his hands again.

"Do you want me to read it to you?" she asked.

Without saying anything, he handed the book back to her and she opened it to the first page.

"My name is Wyatt Thornton," she began. "I am a farm boy from outside Red Oak, Iowa. A couple years ago my best friend, Cory Thatcher moved to Virginia. I thought I would never see him again. But we kept in touch, by texting, instant messaging, by Facebook. He told me about the mountains there and how blue they were.

"We had been in the Future Farmers of America and 4H clubs since we were little and even though he moved to a farm in Virginia with his family, he never, not once, mentioned farming. The only thing he ever talked about now were those mountains. It was as though the mountains awakened something in him that was never there before.

"One day, one of his new friends told him about a mountain trail that ran 500 miles through the state of Virginia. That was the longest trail he had ever heard of until his friend told him that that 500 miles of trail was only a quarter section of the more than 2,100 mile Appalachian Trail that ran from Georgia through Virginia and all the way to Maine.

"'Imagine, Wyatt,' he said to me, 'imagine starting on a mountaintop in Georgia and walking the mountain ridges all the way up to a mountaintop in Maine.'

"Cory told me that as soon as he graduated from high school, he was going to work nine months, save up some money and, in March of the following year, he was going to head to Springer Mountain in Georgia and hike that mountaintop trail to Mount Katahdin in Maine. He told me there wasn't anyone he'd rather do it with than me.

"I told him that hiking for 2000 miles was far to go. I told him that just driving from Red Oak, Iowa to Georgia was also really too far to go just to go walking. Then he said to me that if we ever hiked the trail, that that should be my trail name: Far to Go. Everyone who hikes the A.T. gets a trail name, he said.

"Well, because it was my best friend who was asking me to go, I told him, okay. I would do it. And I would do the same thing that he would do. I would finish high school. I would work until March of the following year and I would hook up with him in Georgia and together we would walk those two thousand miles through forests and rocky slopes and mountain meadows full of wildflowers.

"My friends in Red Oak told me that walking two thousand miles was the craziest thing they had ever heard of. Why would anybody in their right mind want to spend their time and energy doing something like that? And why would you put off going to college for a whole year?

"I had to agree with them. It was crazy. I was also really scared. The more I read about the trail with its ticks, snakes and bears and the stifling heat, the countless days of rain, the less I wanted to do it.

"But according to plans, we both graduated, worked and saved some money. We bought our gear and supplies, and we both set off for Georgia. I waited for hours for Cory to show up at the hotel in Gainesville, but he never came.

"On his way to Georgia, he was in a car accident and broke his leg in three places. I was going to give up the trip and go right up to Virginia to see him but he told me I had better not. He told me that just because he couldn't go doesn't mean I should give up this adventure of a lifetime. He told me it would be the most awesome thing I could ever do for myself. He was right."

Kaitlyn paused and looked up at Collin. She could see he was having a hard time keeping his eyes open. She leaned in close to his face.

"I'll read more, later," she whispered to him.

She placed his book in his hands and he watched her leave the room. No one had ever read to him before.

Collin woke up that evening feeling perfectly fine but very hungry and walked downstairs. Mrs. Meckley fussed over him for getting out of bed, but he did not have even a trace of a temperature.

After he ate supper he went back up to his room and picked up his book to reread the prologue Kaitlyn had read to him that morning.

"Two thousand miles?" Collin said aloud. "Was that guy out of his mind? Why would anybody want to walk two thousand miles?"

Paging through the book, he turned to the very last page and started reading.

"I have finished the journey. I have hiked 2,180 miles from Springer Mountain in Georgia to Katahdin in Maine. I have never felt so alive, so free, so strong. Was it worth it? A thousand times yes. My family and friends still think I am crazy, but that doesn't matter. I started out wanting to do this for my friend Cory, but realized it was something I needed to be doing for me. I have met wonderful and incredible people along the way. I have seen awesome views and stood on mountains I would never have seen if it wasn't for Cory.

"And what about those ticks, snakes, bears, the heat, and the countless days of rain that I had worried about before I even started? Yeah, they were there, but it was okay. I pulled a tick or two off me. I gave the rattlers their space. The couple bears I saw wanted to stay away from me as much as I wanted to stay away from them, the heat was oppressive some days, but it kind of made up for those days I was cold. The rain was no problem either. It made the sunny days all the more beautiful."

Collin closed the book and picked up the atlas from his bookshelf and opened the book to Georgia. He followed the red-dotted line of the Appalachian Trail as it crossed the state border into North Carolina and Tennessee. He saw how it ran diagonally through Virginia, into West Virginia, and north through Maryland, and northeast into Pennsylvania, New Jersey, New York, Connecticut, Massachusetts, Vermont, New Hampshire and finally to Maine.

"You must be nuts!" he said aloud. "Why would you do such a thing? Why would anybody do it?"

He went back to the last page of the book and read aloud the one line that touched him more than any other.

"…I have never felt so alive, so free, so strong…"

He read it again and again.

"I have never felt so alive, so free, so strong."

So free. Yes, Collin said. That's what he wanted. More than anything else, that was what he wanted… to be free. And then he opened the book to the first chapter and started to read.

Chapter 4

As Collin walked into school the next day, he saw everyone was staring at him. It wasn't just his imagination. In the stairwell, in doorways and in the halls, people would point at him and whisper. When he reached his locker he stared back at the group of boys huddled nearby.

"What are you staring at?" he asked in the surly tone he usually reserved when speaking to a teacher or a cop.

"Is that your dad they're talking about on the news?" Tyler Garret, the captain of the football team asked him.

"What are you talking about?" Collin asked them. "My father died when I was little."

"It's all over TV, the newspapers, social media," Tyler continued. "They say some guy by the name of Hunter Talley was going to be executed tonight. They said he was convicted of murdering some people. Maybe he's a relative of yours."

"No," said Collin. "I never heard of the guy."

"But look," a girl called out as she walked over towards them with her smartphone in her hand. "He looks just like you. Look, everybody. Doesn't Collin look like him?"

Collin looked at the picture.

"It doesn't look anything like me," he said, closing his locker. "And like I said, my dad died a long time ago."

As he walked down the hall, he saw everyone had the picture of that man on their phone and they were looking from the picture to Collin and whispering.

Collin was in his first class only five minutes when he was called down to the principal's office.

"What did I do now?" he asked the principal as soon as he saw Mrs. Kintner sitting in a chair inside the room.

"Collin," Mrs. Kintner said rising. "Your father wants to see you."

"No," Collin said. "My dad died a long time ago. Didn't your office tell you anything about me?"

"Son…" Mrs. Kintner started.

"I'm not your son," Collin said.

"Collin," Mrs. Kintner began again. "If you don't want to see him, you don't have to. But later on… you might wish you would have gone."

"I have to go back to class," said Collin heading to the door, but the principal stopped him.

"Give it some thought, Collin," said the principal. "If you decide any time today you want to go, come see me and you can take off."

Yeah, Collin thought, he wouldn't mind getting out of school the rest of the day, but not for this.

Collin went back to class, but his mind was even less focused than ever. When he took the quiz in biology class he signed his name at the top of the page and left the answer lines completely blank. In English Lit, he had his textbook open to a different chapter than the rest of the class. Sometimes when the class turned the page, he would turn a page, too. Sometimes he just sat there staring at nothing.

"Collin," said Mr. Everett. "You okay?"

Collin looked up and was surprised to see the classroom had emptied.

He nodded.

"Did you start the book?" Mr. Everett asked him.

He nodded again, silent for a moment before he began to speak.

"He said he never felt so alive, so free, so strong," Collin said, looking up at his teacher. "He carried a forty-five pound pack on his back for two thousand miles. He walked in snow in North Carolina, and through seven days of non-stop rain in Virginia. He tore up a pair of hiking boots in Pennsylvania and got caught between a mother bear and her cubs in New Jersey, yet he said he never felt so alive, so free, and so strong. I don't get it."

"Collin," the teacher said, more than pleasantly surprised. "Did you… did you read the whole book in one night?"

Collin nodded.

"But I don't get it," Collin said again.

"Well, maybe it's a lot more than just a walk in the woods. Maybe it's about becoming independent and self-sufficient. And being a friend to yourself."

"Being a friend to yourself?"

"Sure," said Everett. "Even though he walked the trail with other hikers some of the time, he was doing the majority of it on his own. When you're by yourself, there's a lot of time for thinking about things. You learn about yourself. You find your strengths and your limitations. You can't hide from yourself out there. When you're out in nature, away from normal everyday things, like television, a computer, supermarkets and cars, you are living in a whole different level of existence. There are no distractions. Finding water, eating, sleeping, the weather… the basic things of living become the most important things in life. There's an inner peace that comes from being out there in the natural world and what better gift to give yourself than that?"

Collin stood up and reached inside his backpack for the book and handed it to his teacher.

"Think you'll ever do it? Hike the trail?" his teacher asked him.

"I think a person would have to be crazy to walk that distance."

"Why don't you keep it?" the teacher said to Collin handing the book back.

Collin shrugged and put it in his pocket. The late bell rang for his next class and Collin looked up at the clock on the wall.

"I'll give you an excuse slip so you don't get into trouble for being late," Mr. Everett said reaching for a small notebook on his desk.

Collin took the slip, but it wasn't necessary. He had no intention of going to his next class. He stashed his pack in his locker and walked down to the principal's office.

When Mrs. Kintner drove him up to the front gate of the prison, Collin did not expect to see the crowd of protestors congregated there. He also did not expect the glaring lights of news cameras placed at different points throughout the crowd.

When the car was stopped at the gate, a cameraman, only a few feet from the car window, focused directly on Collin. A light flashed a moment before the car was waved through.

Collin soon found himself entering the maximum-security prison. They took his jacket, frisked him, and then made him empty his pockets.

"Your book and your jacket will be returned to you on your way out," said one of the guards.

They led Collin through a maze of halls and long corridors. Every door they went through had to be unlocked and locked as soon as they passed through it. It was the most claustrophobic and depressing place he had ever seen and far worse than any of the places he had been in as a child.

Finally he was led to a small room with a glass partition and told to wait.

Two minutes later they brought a man in handcuffs into the room.

Collin and the man stared at each other from across the glass partition. They had not seen each other in almost thirteen years.

"I'd have known you anywhere," said the man. "I'm glad you came."

Collin didn't say anything. He didn't know this man. There were only vague shadowy memories that had all but faded away.

"You doing good in school?" the man asked.

"Yeah," said Collin, as surly as he could. "Straight A's."

But the man saw through his lie.

"Son, I made a lot of mistakes," the man began. "I'm sorry I wasn't there for you. I'm sorry things have turned out like this. The family you are with, they treating you okay?"

"What if they aren't?" Collin asked. "What are you going to do about it?"

The man was silent then spoke again.

"Be a good boy. Be a good man. When you find someone to love, love them with all your heart. Don't ever do anything to change that. Don't ever do anything to hurt the ones you love… When you're a kid, sometimes you do stupid things. Please don't ever do anything so stupid that can't be undone. Please, be good. Do you hear me, Collin?"

Collin nodded.

"Promise me?"

"Yeah, whatever," said Collin.

"Take care of yourself, son."

The man stood up and was gone.

For a moment Collin stared at the prison door his father had gone through.

"You okay?" a prison guard asked him.

"Get me out of here," said Collin standing up. "I don't know why I came. I don't even know him."

Collin was led back out to the front office where Mrs. Kintner was waiting for him.

"Here," she said, handing him a pair of sunglasses. "Put these on."

As they drove past the media at the gate, Collin heard them shouting his name, and yelling questions to him about his father. But Mrs. Kintner gunned the engine and they drove quickly away from the frenzied mob and bright lights and rode back to Kepner Creek in silence.

The following morning Collin's picture was on the front page of the Kepner Creek newspaper. It was the lead story on every television channel and social media site. The headline blared, "Condemned Man Sees Teen Son Final Time."

"You *are* Hunter Talley's son," a girl at school said to Collin as she flashed his picture at the prison gate on her smartphone to everyone as they gathered at Collin's locker.

"You little liar," said Tyler. "You said he died years ago."

Collin didn't even open his locker. He turned around, walked down the hall and right out of the building.

After he left school, Collin ran the three miles to his place near the highway. A convoy of trucks was heading east. Two recreational vehicles were heading west and countless hundreds of cars were heading in both directions.

He looked east and he looked west. Which way should he go? West was California, east was New York. New York was cold and gray. California was warm and sunny and had beaches.

He stood at the highway and stuck out his thumb. In minutes a car pulled over and stopped.

"Where are you heading?" the driver asked.

Collin stood there silently staring at the driver. This was his opportunity. He could go anywhere.

"Do you want a lift or don't you?" the driver asked.

When the boy didn't respond the driver took off. Slowly Collin backed away from the highway and headed for home.

No one was there when he entered the house. He went into Mr. Meckley's office and searched the internet for the one thing he wanted. He printed the page and wrote a note on it before leaving it on his desk.

If you want to get me something for my birthday, this is what I want. Collin

He went out to the shed, jumped on the small tractor and tilled the garden until Mrs. Meckley drove up the driveway with her children.

"You've been busy, I see," said Mrs. Meckley, as she lifted out two bags of groceries.

Collin took the bags from her.

“Thank you,” she said. “I’ll get the other two.”

He carried the bags to the kitchen and started unpacking the groceries, loading them onto the pantry shelves.

“How does fried chicken and mashed potatoes sound for supper?” she asked.

“Yayyy,” the kids yelled.

“All right,” said Mrs. Meckley. “Kids, go and wash up for dinner. I want to talk to Collin.”

Mrs. Meckley waited until the children left before she spoke.

“I guess you saw the news reports today,” she began.

He nodded.

“I think the media can be very heartless. Are you okay?”

He shrugged.

“The principal called and said you had left school. He said he didn’t expect you to be there at all today, but he heard what the kids were saying. Oh, Collin, I’m sorry. I can’t imagine how hard it was for you.”

“I’m not going back there,” he told her.

“Collin, I know kids’ teasing is a cruel thing, but we must all do things we don’t like to do. You must go back tomorrow or else they will take you away from here.”

Collin knew he had no choice. Being there was better than being locked up.

“It will be all right,” she said, patting his shoulder. “You’ll see.”

He went back to school the following morning and was stopped at his locker.

"Yeah, Collin's dad is quite a celebrity," one boy taunted. "He's been in the news nonstop."

"Yeah?" asked another mockingly. "For what? For sports? Is he the one who signed that million dollar contract?"

"No," said the first boy.

"Was he that successful financial genius on Wall Street?"

"No."

"Then it must have been in the entertainment field for winning an Oscar," the second boy said.

"Oh, it was entertainment all right," said another. "But that loser won nothing but a one way ticket to…"

He was cut short when a teacher opened his classroom door and poked his head out.

"Boys, what's going on here?" Mr. Everett spoke up.

"Nothing, Mr. Everett," one student said. "Just heading for homeroom."

"Keep moving and keep the noise down."

Collin grabbed his books and headed for his homeroom wondering how long he could handle staying in school, wondering how long he could hold back his anger before his fist would land on those harassing him. He knew it was only a matter of time before someone was going to get hurt.

At lunchtime Collin bought a candy bar from the vending machine and went to the library instead of eating lunch in the cafeteria.

He opened the book, *Walking the High Mountain Ridge,* to midway through the first chapter.

On the trail you can have a whole different persona from your life in the so-called real world. You can remain anonymous to everyone. That is one of the reasons why hikers take on a trail name instead of using their real name. Sometimes it's the other long distance hikers who give you your trail name. Sometimes you pick the name yourself.

Anonymous to everyone, Collin thought. Yeah, that would be a very good thing. No one would know he was the son of the executed, convicted murderer Hunter Talley. He would be someone else. He could be anyone he wanted to be. He could be… His mind drew a blank. He did not know what name to pick.

"The name will come," Collin said to himself. "It will come. It's only a matter of time."

Collin found refuge in the school library every day after that. He was alone to read and think and wonder. One afternoon when he was reading about the Appalachian Trail in the White Mountains of New Hampshire, two boys from his class came in and stood at his table.

Rumors were running like wildfire through school about Collin and the crimes he supposedly had committed before coming to Kepner Creek.

"So that's what a murderer's son looks like," said the first boy.

"Yeah," said the second. "Ugly… just like his father."

"They said they never found the weapon from that last killing he did." The first boy pointed to Collin and said to his friend, "Do you think he has it?"

Collin wanted them to shut up and leave him alone. They started it and if he kept silent, they would never stop.

Collin stood up and slowly reached into his pocket.

"Keep talking stupid like that and you'll find out soon enough," Collin said in a voice that told them he was not joking around.

Scenes of violence and tragedy at other schools in other towns flashed through the first boy's mind.

"Let's get out of here," he said to his friend, certain that Collin had a weapon in his pocket.

The second boy backed away as well, and they both ran out of the library.

Collin smiled, pleased that it took so little intimidation from him for them to go away. From his pocket he pulled a wadded-up candy wrapper, threw it away in the trash can and returned to his seat.

But in less than fifteen minutes, the principal, followed by the deputy, entered the library.

"Stand up," said the deputy. "Keep your hands up and in plain sight."

Collin was pushed against a bookshelf and was searched, while the principal picked up Collin's backpack and dumped its contents on the table.

"Aren't you going to ask what's going on?" the deputy asked Collin.

"Does it matter?" Collin asked him. "You're going to do what you want to do anyway."

"Did you bring a knife or a gun with you into school?" the deputy asked.

"No," said Collin, extremely upset. "Why would you think that?"

"We had a report that you did."

Collin looked at the principal.

"You're making me late for my next class," Collin said to him. "Can I go now?"

"Not so fast," said the deputy. "I must check your locker."

Collin shook his head. Even the deputy and the principal were believing the rumors. He had no criminal record. He had no contact with his father when his father committed his crimes.

"Take your things with you," said the deputy.

Collin put his books back in his pack and went with the deputy and principal to his locker. The bell rang and students streamed into the hall just as the deputy was searching it.

"Keep moving," the principal said to them.

"It's clean," said the deputy closing the locker.

"You may go to your next class now," the principal said to Collin. "But know this, we're watching you."

"Yeah, I see that," said Collin in exasperation, staring at both the deputy and the principal and, just behind them, a wall of students.

Chapter 5

For two weeks, Collin listened to the cruel words of his classmates. He kept silent, not talking back, not defending himself.

When his birthday came, Collin forgot them momentarily as he opened his presents.

"Happy Birthday, Collin," said Mr. Meckley, handing the biggest gift on the table to Collin first.

Collin opened up the package. It was just what he wanted. A brand new backpack. It was the exact kind Wyatt "Far to Go" Thornton used on his Appalachian Trail thru-hike.

"Thanks," Collin said. When he had left the picture of the backpack on Mr. Meckley's desk two weeks ago, he didn't expect to actually receive one.

"You're welcome, but we didn't buy it. It's a present from Curtis Everett."

Wow, he thought to himself, his teacher buying something like that for him!

The Meckleys gave Collin some shirts, some money and one last box. Opening it he found a pair of hiking boots in his size.

"We figured if you were going to need the backpack," said Mrs. Meckley, "you would also need a good pair of hiking boots. They're waterproof and they have these rugged, lug soles made special for traction on steep slopes."

Collin put them on. They fit great.

"Thanks," he said again.

He took his presents up to his room and put on his big pack, trying it out for size. Staring in the mirror, he held up *Walking the High Mountain Ridge* and compared how he looked to Wyatt 'Far to Go' Thornton's picture on the front cover.

"I am a hiker, too," he said. Taking off his big pack, he put his book inside it.

There was nothing to hold him here in Kepner Creek now. He could head out any time, hitch a ride on the interstate and head for Springer Mountain in Georgia.

The next day was Friday. Before leaving for school, Collin picked up his small school backpack and looked down at his new one. The small pack, dwarfed by his real trail backpack, now looked like a kid's toy. He couldn't wait to use the new one on the trail.

Collin went to school, but even before he reached the building, he was stopped by a carload of kids in the parking lot. They surrounded him before he could get away.

"You know, what your father did wasn't right," said Tyler, the largest one of the group.

"You're right," said Collin.

"He got what he deserved."

"He did." Collin stated.

"Hey, how come you're agreeing with what I'm saying?"

"Because it's true," Collin told him.

"But that's your father. How come you're not defending him?"

"I haven't seen him since I was two. I don't remember him. Now he's gone forever. And nothing anybody says or does will bring him or any of those people back."

"What about the gun they never found?" someone in the back of the crowd yelled. "He probably has it in his pack."

"Would you stop it," Collin sighed, tired of their accusations. "I don't have anything."

But they wouldn't stop. They wouldn't leave him alone.

When Tyler tried to take Collin's pack full of books, Collin lost it and threw the first punch. He tried to back away after he took Tyler down, but he was knocked off his feet by the rest of the group.

"Fight," someone yelled and suddenly fists were flying.

Teachers came streaming from the building. By the time everyone was pulled apart, everyone, including the deputy arriving on the scene, saw a knife lying beside Collin's backpack.

"Why did I know you were going to be in the middle of this?" the deputy asked Collin, hauling him to his feet.

"They started it," Collin told the deputy as he wiped blood away from his nose and mouth.

"Sure they did," said the deputy. "And who was the one that pulled this out?" The deputy reached down and picked up the knife.

"It wasn't me," said Collin. "I hope you dust it for fingerprints, because you won't find any of mine on it."

The deputy put the knife away and pulled out a pair of handcuffs.

"You have the right to remain silent," he said as he gripped Collin's wrist.

"Why do you all have to keep doing this to me?" Collin asked the lawman.

For one moment the deputy hesitated, with the handcuffs down by his side. He never saw anyone looking so distraught. But in the next instant, Collin broke away from his grasp, took off out of the parking lot and disappeared into the fields behind the school.

Collin hid out until dark. Long after midnight he sneaked into the Meckley house after everyone was asleep. Going to his room he threw his clothes into his brand new backpack and changed into his brand new hiking boots. He stuffed his money into his pocket and sat down at his desk. Tearing out a sheet of paper from his notebook, he grabbed a pen and quickly wrote a letter.

Dear Mr. and Mrs. Meckley,

Thanks for taking me in. I know you tried hard to help me. But I don't belong here. Things have been getting worse and worse at school. Why can't they just leave me alone? I haven't done anything wrong and now they say I had a knife. I can't do this any more. I can't. And I don't want to be locked up for something I didn't do, so I'm leaving. Don't try to find me. *Collin Talley*

He put the note on his desk, grabbed his jacket, his backpack with his copy of *Walking the High Mountain Ridge*, and left.

After taking his familiar route to the interstate and his place under the billboard one last time, he stood on the highway. This was it. He was on his way.

He had no trouble hitching a ride. A big tractor trailer rig pulled over almost immediately.

"Where are you heading?" Collin asked the trucker.

"Florida."

"Perfect," said Collin hopping in. "I'm trying to get to Georgia."

"I don't see many people out this time of night, and definitely not anyone as young as you."

"Yeah, well, an emergency came up," said Collin without elaborating.

"How old are you?"

"Eighteen," Collin lied.

The trucker didn't ask anything further, but Collin could tell he was wondering about him.

An hour later the trucker pulled into a rest stop near Omaha.

"I gotta get some coffee. Need anything?"

"No," said Collin.

"I'll be right back."

Collin watched the man cross the parking lot and head into the convenience store. Though he was glad for the ride, Collin was so anxious to be on his way he hoped the trucker would be quick.

Collin checked out the dashboard of the big rig and noticed the clock. It was three a.m. He had been up all day and now all night and he knew it was going to be a long haul until he could find a place to get some sleep. Right now, though, he had to stay awake and alert.

He considered momentarily closing his eyes for a few minutes until he heard voices and looked out to see the trucker coming across the parking lot with a cop.

"I know he must be a runaway," Collin could hear the trucker telling the cop. "He's too young to be out on the highway."

Collin grabbed his pack and slipped out the driver's side door into the early morning darkness, hiding until the trucker pulled out and the cop left.

It wasn't until after dawn that Collin caught a ride in an SUV. They crossed out of Nebraska and into Iowa. The miles were now flying by. The state of Illinois came and went and then, Indiana. Morning became afternoon.

Outside of Toledo, Ohio, the driver dropped him off at one of the rest stops on the Interstate.

"This is probably the best place for finding a ride south," the driver said. Then, with a quick good-bye, the driver was gone.

Tired and hungry, Collin grabbed a soda at the rest stop.

And then he waited with his thumb out. And he waited some more. No one was stopping. He was living his nightmare of standing by the side of the road unable to get anyone to pull over.

He had been up two whole days and a night. Now evening of the second night was approaching. He needed sleep desperately, but more so, he needed to start heading south.

It was after dark when finally a truck pulled over.

"You heading south?" Collin asked him.

"North Carolina," the driver answered.

Collin hopped inside the cab.

The steady hum of the motor and the long road was lulling Collin to sleep. He kept trying to fight it, but in less than an hour he was out.

When next he awoke he had no idea where he was.

"Where are we?" Collin asked the trucker.

"Sorry, kid. I had a slight change of plans. I have to go to Boston to pick up a load."

"Boston? But that's north."

"Yeah," said the trucker.

"So, where are we?" Collin asked, nervously.

"We're in Pennsylvania."

"Pennsylvania?"

"Yeah, for a few hours now. Route 80."

"No," said Collin, shaking his head in frustration. "You have to let me out. I have to go south. Why didn't you wake me up?"

"Believe me, kid, I tried to," said the trucker, "but you were sleeping so soundly, I thought you were drugged. I couldn't just throw you out on the side of the road while you were sleeping and I couldn't call a cop because I'd get in trouble for having you inside my rig. Look, we're coming up to 81. That will head south."

The trucker pulled over at the intersecting highway in the middle of the night.

"Take care, kid. Good luck to you."

Collin walked for over an hour but no one would stop to give him a lift. When he saw a Pennsylvania state cop car approaching, Collin cut across a field and walked along a backcountry road. No cars even passed him until dawn.

The first car that came by stopped and offered him a lift.

"I'm heading for Pottsville," the driver said.

"Is that south of here?" Collin asked.

"Sure is."

"Great, thanks for stopping."

When they reached the town, Collin jumped out.

Across the highway Collin saw a fast food restaurant. He only had a little money in his pocket that he wanted to hold on to as long as he could, but he was hungry now. He bought one hamburger and went to look for another ride.

"I'm heading for Strausstown," said a man who pulled over in a jeep.

"Is that south?" Collin asked.

"Yeah, it's south."

"Good," said Collin, hopping inside. "Thanks for stopping."

"Sure thing. Looks like you're going hiking."

"Yeah. I'm trying to get to Georgia to hike the Appalachian Trail."

"That trail goes all the way down there?" the man asked.

"It starts in Georgia," said Collin feeling like an expert. "And it goes to Maine."

"Yeah, now that you mention it, I've seen the sign for it on the road up ahead. The Appalachian Trail cuts right across Route 183."

"We're going to go past it?" Collin asked.

"Yeah, I'll slow down when we get there. I've seen hikers crossing the road. Sometimes scout troops."

Yeah, thought Collin, of course it goes through Pennsylvania. It just surprised him that he was this close to it.

They drove on for several miles in silence.

"My name's Mark," the driver said. "I didn't catch your name."

"Collin."

"So tell me, Collin, your folks are letting you do this all by yourself?"

"I'm eighteen," Collin lied. "I can take care of myself."

"Yeah," said the man, staring at the bruises on Collin's face. "I see. And I was born yesterday. You don't look a day over fourteen, maybe fifteen. You should call your folks and let them know you're all right."

"My folks are dead and the people I was with won't miss me."

"I won't turn you in," said the man pulling out a business card. "But here, take my card. If you ever need anything, especially when you get back up to Pennsylvania, give me a call and let me know how you're making out. Okay?"

"Thanks," said Collin. I guess this is what "Far to Go" meant by trail magic, he thought to himself. Someone was doing something nice and he wasn't even officially on the trail yet. Yeah, this hiking the Appalachian Trail was going to be a good thing. No, an awesome thing. And he couldn't wait.

The car went down one hill and before it climbed up the next one, Collin looked up. There, directly in front of them, was a vast green mountain.

"This is the Blue Mountain," the driver told him. "It looks green up close, but from a distance it looks blue."

As they arrived at the curve on the crest of the hill, the driver pulled into the small parking area to their right.

"This is it," the driver said. "This here is the Appalachian Trail."

Collin looked off to his right and saw how the trail passed by an iron gate and disappeared into the trees and then he looked to his left to see where it continued on the other side of the road.

Mark motioned across the road and pointed to the sign.

"See it," he said, reading it. "The Appalachian Trail, Maine to Georgia."

This was really it, Collin thought as he stared at the sign. To the left was Maine. To the right, was the way to Georgia. He had to get out of the car and see the sign up close.

"Are you in a hurry?" Collin asked. "Can you give me a second to check it out?"

Mark smiled.

"Go ahead, kid, I got a couple minutes."

Collin grabbed his pack and put it on as he waited for the road to be clear of cars. He then ran over to the sign and touched it. This was it. This was the Appalachian Trail.

He looked north on the trail. It went up a little embankment and headed through the trees. He was about to take his first step on it when he paused.

No, he wouldn't do it just yet. In a couple months he would be back here after having walked to this point from Georgia. He would not encroach on even an inch of it until he did the whole thing from the beginning.

Yeah, he thought to himself. More than anything, he had to get to Georgia. He waved to the man to let him know he was coming and ran out onto the empty road.

He heard a horn and in an instant he saw something red flying straight towards him. Instinctively, he put out his hand as if he could stop it.

For a moment there was incredible pain and he felt himself sailing through the air and then there was nothing.

Chapter 6

There were screams coming from the front passenger seat of the shiny, brand new, candy-apple red Audi roadster convertible as it careened around the curve in the road and struck the hiker. The car spun out of control and stopped backwards on the paved median.

"Oh my God, Brooke," Jason screamed. "You hit him. You hit him."

"Get a grip," said Brooke. "He ran right into the road. It was his fault."

"You were going like forty miles over the speed limit, Brooke," Jason yelled.

"Didn't you hear me? I said it wasn't my fault."

They jumped out of the car.

"Look at my car," she screamed hysterically. "Look at it. I just got it and look at it."

"Brooke," Jason said, putting his arm around her. "Would you shut up! Are you out of your mind? You just hit somebody and look…" He pointed to the cameras. "Everyone is watching."

Brooke turned to see photographers filming everything she was saying and everything that had just happened.

"Turn that camera off. It's your fault," Brooke yelled to them. "You were chasing me."

"No, you were speeding," said one of the cameramen. "Nobody but you was driving that car. Nobody but you hit that guy."

"Look, it wasn't my fault!" she screamed to them. "And I don't have to be here. Jason, I'm out of here. Are you coming?"

"Brooke," he said, stopping her from getting back in her car. "What are you doing? You can't leave. You hit somebody. Did you even check to see if he's alive?"

They glanced where the hiker lay on the opposite side of the road, thirty feet away from where he was struck. Other drivers had already pulled over and were surrounding the still form on the macadam.

"Why?" Brooke said, loud enough for the camera crews to hear and record her. "Why should I check him? Do I look like a doctor? I'm out of here."

"You can't," said Jason again.

"Yes, I can. C'mon Jase, let's go."

"I don't know, Brooke. I don't think you ought to be going anywhere."

"That's right you're not," said Mark, the man from the car parked by the side of the road. He left Collin's side when he saw she was trying to leave. Grabbing the keys from her hand, he threw them into the woods.

"You can't do that," she screamed. "You don't know who I am."

"I can't?" said the man. "Looks like I already did."

"I'm calling the police," said Brooke. "And then I'm calling my father."

"The police are already on the way," someone from the camera crew called to her.

Brooke grabbed her smart phone.

Laura hurry up and get here, she texted.

Her friend, Laura, unable to keep up with Brooke's fast speed, was somewhere behind her.

Mark hurried back over to Collin while one of the cameramen followed him.

"Who are you?" Mark asked the crewman. "What are you all doing here?"

"We're with WHBH, you know, Harrisburg Hot. Those other guys in those vans are part of the regular paparazzi that follows Brooke Setree."

"Nope, don't know you. Don't know that girl either, but I'm real glad you're here."

"You don't know Brooke Setree?" the crewman asked, startled that the man had no clue of who was in their midst. "That's Senator John Gordon Setree's daughter who just hit that kid. She's *the* party girl, *the* socialite. She's always in the news. Who's the kid that got hit?"

"Just a kid I gave a ride to."

Mark bent down to see if Collin was breathing.

"Geez, there's a lot of blood," said Mark. He looked up at the cameraman. "Must you do that? Can't you turn that thing off? The kid's bleeding."

The cameraman called to his assistant who was already running over with a first aid kit.

"We shouldn't move him," Mark said, "but we gotta get this pack off him and try to stop the bleeding."

Somewhere far away Collin heard yelling. Distant yelling. But somehow people were close by. He opened his eyes, but couldn't see. He was face down on the roadway and he tried, but couldn't get up.

"Don't try to move," a voice called to him. "The ambulance is coming."

Ten minutes later Brooke's friend arrived. Turning her back on Jason, Brooke jumped into her friend's car. She wanted to get as far away from this place as she could. This was her birthday after all. And her brand new car was wrecked. As soon as she could get a hold of her father, she would see to it that all the paparazzi, all the cameramen and crew, and the news station they worked for were sued for all they were worth for invading her privacy.

"Hey, where is she going?" someone called.

"She's taking off," said one of the crewmen. "She just got in that car. You stay here and keep filming. I'll follow her."

Collin tried to push himself up, but all he could do was lift one arm. There was a pain that burned so intensely in his side and chest that he could not breathe.

"What happened?" he asked in a whisper.

"You got hit by a car," Mark said, gently touching Collin's shoulder.

"What happened?" he asked again.

The man knew from his repeated question that Collin was suffering from a head injury.

"Hold on," said Mark. "Do you hear me? You hold on. The ambulance is coming."

"I can't breathe," Collin gasped.

"You're going to be okay," Mark said, trying to reassure the boy.

But in the midst of his injuries Collin knew he wasn't going to be okay. Something was terribly wrong. He couldn't breathe and he couldn't see because of the blood running down his face.

There were sirens loud and close and someone was saying they were going to cut his pack off.

No, thought Collin just before he passed out. Please don't cut my backpack.

He remembered nothing of the helicopter ride to the trauma center. Faces and bright lights seemed to float in and out of his consciousness.

"Can you tell us your name?" someone asked him when he opened his eyes.

"What happened?" was all Collin could whisper.

"You were in a car accident," he was told. "But don't you worry, we're going to take good care of you and you're going to be okay. Can you tell us your name?"

The pressure in his chest was unbearable; he could scarcely get a breath in or out. The pain in his head and his arm was excruciating and for a moment Collin knew this was what it felt like to die.

"Son, can you tell us your name?"

"I found it," someone said, holding up his book. "It says Curtis Everett. Kepner Creek, Nebraska."

"We'll call your folks, Curtis. They're going to take you up to the operating room now."

Collin felt a stabbing pain and then there was nothing.

It was a long time until he opened his eyes.

"Can you hear me, Collin?" a woman's voice asked.

Collin nodded.

"You're in the Trauma Center. You're going to be okay."

They always told you that, Collin knew, even if you weren't. There was a tube in his mouth and he wanted to ask them what happened. When Collin tried to raise his broken arm to look at it, the nurse seemed to know what he wanted.

"You were hit by a car," said the nurse. "Your left arm and three ribs are broken. One of the ribs punctured your lung. You have a concussion and numerous cuts and contusions on your face which will heal in time."

In time? It must be pretty bad, Collin thought. He tried to touch his face but the nurse stopped him.

"The plastic surgeon said you will be fine," the nurse continued, "but you must keep your hands off your face."

The next days were surreal; time seemed suspended while he lay immobilized with the worst headache he ever had.

"Where's my backpack?" was the first question he asked when his brain cleared.

"I don't know," the nurse said to him.

"Did they get the person who did this?" Collin whispered.

"Don't talk now," said the nurse. "Just rest."

One afternoon a man came to see him. Collin knew where he was from even before he introduced himself.

"I am Jeff Dillon from the Schuylkill County Youth Services. I will be your caseworker while you are in the hospital and until you are transferred to our county Juvenile Corrections Center."

"No," said Collin. "I'm staying with the Meckleys."

"I'm afraid that is no longer an option for you," said the caseworker very matter-of-factly. "The state of Nebraska has relinquished their authority over you.

You are now a ward of the Commonwealth of Pennsylvania."

Mrs. Kintner and the judge had warned him what would happen and now he was helpless to do anything about it.

"But you don't understand..." Collin began to say.

He only left Kepner Creek because he was going to be falsely arrested for carrying a knife. He had to run away.

"Take it easy," said Jeff. "We'll talk later."

No, Collin thought. He didn't want to talk to this man now or at any later time. Collin knew he must leave, before they could take him into custody.

He waited until the caseworker left and he was alone. Now was his chance. But the moment he tried to stand up, he fainted.

A week after he was hit by the car he was released from the hospital and remanded to the Schuylkill County Juvenile Corrections Center. Because of his injuries, he was sent directly to the infirmary and isolated from the rest of the population. And there he sat all alone.

"I didn't think I'd be in solitary confinement," he said aloud, but there was no one to hear him.

He lay down and slept a while, then got up and looked out the door. There was no one in the outer room so he tried the handle on that door. He was surprised when it opened. He tried the door to the outside hallway, but that one was locked.

He paged through some three-year-old magazines sitting on the table in the small lounge area. Then he saw the television in the corner and picked up the remote that was sitting on top of it and turned it on.

He went through all three hundred channels and could pick up only three. The first was a documentary on snails. The second was a cooking channel. The third was a political talk show.

"I don't see how Senator Setree thinks he has a chance to win the Presidency this November," said the one commentator.

"His platform is solid," said the other political analyst.

"But in light of his daughter's most recent actions, how can he think he can take control of the country, if he has no control over his own daughter?"

"It was just an adolescent action, a phase, if you will. And we can't judge the Senator over something a juvenile relative did. This has happened in the past, time and again, and should have no reflection on the president and his leadership abilities."

"An adolescent action? A juvenile relative? It was his daughter! She was speeding. She hit a boy and she left the scene. That is not just an adolescent prank. It was a hit and run. That is a crime. The viewers can judge for themselves and call in with their comments."

As the commentator finished talking, the footage of what they were discussing rolled across the screen.

Collin watched as the camera crew followed the speeding red convertible.

"We are going over eighty miles an hour in a forty-five mile per hour speed zone," said one of the reporters. "And we are just barely keeping up with Senator and Presidential hopeful John Gordon Setree's daughter, Brooke Setree. Miss Setree just turned 16 today. She's a new driver with a brand new car and she is out of control. Miss Setree has been joy riding for nearly an hour now since leaving her home in Harrisburg and why she has not been stopped before this is amazing. We haven't even seen any police cars. She was going twenty miles over the speed limit on the interstate, weaving in and out of traffic. But now she's flying up Route 183 at close to ninety miles an hour. We just passed Route 419 and we're still climbing up the mountain."

There was silence for a moment and then the reporter yelled.

"Oh my God! She just hit someone on the curve. She just hit someone! Did you see that? Pull over, pull over. Call an ambulance."

Collin slowly moved closer to the screen. He couldn't believe what he was seeing. He was the guy who got hit and went flying through the air. He watched as he landed hard, face down on the roadway.

"I can't believe this," he said aloud as he watched the film of himself getting hit… hit by a senator's daughter. "That's me."

"You should sue them," said someone behind Collin.

Collin looked up at the trusty, a fellow prisoner, a year or two older than himself, who was carrying a tray of food into the room for Collin.

"Nobody told me about this," Collin said.

"Of course not. They never do. Do you think she'll spend one day in a place like this? Hell, no! Her father's rich. He's running for president. You'll never hear from them."

And then they watched as Brooke Setree ranted and raved about her car.

"It wasn't my fault," she said. "Look at my car. Look at it. I just got it and look at it."

Collin stood right by the screen looking in disbelief at the girl.

"Such callous disregard for the person she hit," said one of the commentators on the show. "Is this the kind of attitude we want running our country for the next four years?"

Collin kept his eyes on the screen as they showed him lying in a pool of blood on the macadam. He watched as his brand new backpack was cut off his back.

"Oh, man, they cut my pack," Collin whispered. "They totally wrecked it. It was brand new. I never even got to use it."

"Our lines are open," said the commentator. "Please give us a call."

Collin looked around and spotted a telephone on the desk.

"You have to dial nine to get out," the trusty told him.

"Thanks," said Collin as he dialed the number on the screen.

He had to only wait a moment when someone answered the phone.

"The World At Large, what is your topic?" the operator asked.

"My name is Collin Talley. That senator's daughter hit me with her car."

"Are you really Collin Talley?" the operator asked him.

"They ruined my backpack," he practically shouted. "They had to cut it off. I never even got to use it."

"Can you hold? I'll put the call right through. They'll want to talk to you."

"Do you know they'll make you hang up if they catch you on the phone?" the trusty said.

"Can you watch the door?" Collin asked him.

His fellow inmate nodded.

"This is the World At Large," Collin heard a voice say on both the phone and the television. "Collin, how are you doing?"

He didn't know where to start.

"Look, I can't talk long," he began. "I'm locked up in the Schuylkill County Juvenile Corrections Center. They brought me here from the hospital and they didn't even let me talk to a lawyer. I didn't do anything wrong. Is that girl who hit me in jail? I bet she isn't. Look, I don't know anything about politics. And I suppose the senator's daughter will get a chance to go on living her life. But all I want is a chance, too."

"Somebody's coming," said Collin's lookout.

"I have to go," he said and hung up the phone.

Quickly he switched off the television and wondered if his call made any difference at all.

It did.

Signs along the Appalachian Trail in Pennsylvania help guide hikers to shelters, road crossings and other trails.

Chapter 7

Before the day was over, two lawyers came to see Collin Talley and brought with them a court order for his release into their custody.

"Collin," said the first lawyer, "I am Casey Dare. You are going to come and stay with us until the court hearing. This is my husband, Michael."

"You can call me Mike," he said. "We have a lot to do before the hearing. But first we need some good publicity. Are you up for appearing on television?"

"Yeah, sure, I guess," said Collin. "But, what for?"

"What the senator's daughter did was not right," said Casey, "and she needs to answer for it. Her parents need to be held accountable."

"Her father needs to be held accountable," Mike stressed. "He needs to address this. If he doesn't show some responsibility for his daughter's actions now, his approval rating will go down. If he can't handle his own daughter, then how can he possibly handle running the whole country?"

"I take it you won't be voting for him," said Collin.

Mike glanced at Casey and for a moment they said nothing.

"It doesn't matter if we are for him or against him," said Mike. "Damage has been done. We're going to make it right."

They drove Collin to their office and he sat in a large stuffed leather chair in the corner of an equally large conference room while ten different people sat at the table talking about writs and precedence and corpus delicti and which judge might hear the case. They babbled on to infinity about the Senator and his people and what angle they were going to use with the media.

Collin thought they would never stop talking. His head was throbbing, his arm and side hurt, and he was hungry. He closed his eyes and rested his head on his arm, but continued to listen as best as he could.

"The immediate job will be to prep our client for the media events and then focus on the hearing. We have to keep the public sympathetic to him. We do that by focusing on his injuries and then contrast that with Miss Setree's rants. We need to mention he's an orphan, but don't bring up anything about truancy or being a runaway."

"But they already know he's from Nebraska," said another voice. "They already know about his father. How do we explain a fifteen year old kid from Nebraska standing on a road in Pennsylvania? Really, what was he doing there?"

They all looked over to Collin for an explanation.

Collin heard the room fall silent. Thank God, he thought, they were finally done talking. He opened his eyes and saw everyone was staring at him.

"Perhaps we need to pick this up in the morning," said Casey. "It's been a long day."

Casey and her husband took Collin home with them. They showed him their guest room where he would stay, then invited him into the kitchen while they cooked dinner. After they ate they told Collin they wanted to talk to him.

"We'll go in the library," said Mike.

Collin sat down in the large chair closest to the fireplace and watched as Mike started a fire and added some logs to it.

"First thing in the morning we'll go clothes shopping," said Casey, "but if there's anything you need tonight, just ask."

"Can I call someone?"

"Sure," said Casey handing him her phone.

"I don't know their number."

"Who do you want to call?" she asked.

"The family I was staying with."

"Oh, the Meckleys," Mike said as he reached for his laptop and opened up one of his files. He turned the screen to Collin. "I have that number. Here you go."

"How did you know their name?" Collin asked.

"We did a little research on you," he said.

"Yeah? And did your research show if they'll hang up on me if I try to call them?"

"Our research shows," Casey spoke up, "that they would be happy to hear that you are okay."

He called their number and Kate answered.

"Mrs. Meckley," he began. "It's me, Collin."

"Collin, thank God you're okay! The news kept showing that crazy girl hitting you. They showed it again and again and we thought you were dead."

"I'm sorry I ran away. That deputy was going to arrest me for having a knife, but it wasn't mine."

"Yes, we know. Ty admitted it was his. He saw what happened to you on the news and he went right down to the deputy and told him the knife was his and that you didn't do anything wrong."

"Looks like I'm going to be here a while. They told me that I'm a ward of Pennsylvania now, that Nebraska doesn't want me. Some lawyers got me out of jail, but there's supposed to be a hearing. I don't know what's going to happen, but I just wanted to say thanks for everything you and your family did for me. I have to go now."

"You take care, Collin. We'll be thinking of you."

Collin handed the phone back to Casey.

"Collin," Mike began. "What were you doing on the road when you got hit?"

"I was looking at that sign," he began, but quickly changed his thoughts. "You know, I don't remember getting hit. I just remember waking up and I couldn't breathe."

"What sign are you talking about?" Mike asked.

"The Appalachian Trail sign," he said, but again changed the subject. "I don't know why this had to happen. I wasn't supposed to be in Pennsylvania."

"We'll get to that," Casey said. "We want to know what you were doing there on that road."

"What?" he asked, looking at them both. What was it they didn't understand?

"It was a sign for the Appalachian Trail," he said, trying to explain it to them. "And I just wanted to see it up close, because it was there. It was right there."

From their silence, Collin realized that they didn't get it.

"See," he began again. "I didn't think I would see the Appalachian Trail until I got to Georgia. That's where I wanted to go, to Georgia, to start it from the very beginning. That was my plan, but nothing ever works out. All the rides I got were heading east, not south. Pennsylvania… that's like midway on the trail and I didn't want to start it in the middle. But there we were at that trail crossing and I just wanted to see that sign up close."

"So, you were planning on hiking. Do you really want to do the whole trail?" Mike asked him.

"Yes," said Collin.

"But why?" Mike continued. "That doesn't seem like it would be an easy thing to do. It seems it would be a journey fraught with challenges and deprivation."

"Yeah," said his wife. "Backpacking is a tough way to travel. You have to carry everything you need with you. There's no indoor plumbing, no heating or air conditioning."

"Deprivation?" Collin said, getting to his feet. Were they for real? "Carrying everything you need?" These people seemed so clueless.

"I'm fifteen years old," he began, "and do you know what I have?"

He looked down at the clothes he was wearing.

"This. This is it. This ugly, old, worn, juvie issued uniform. This is all I have."

"Didn't you have things at the Meckley home?"

"They gave me clothes. They were in my pack, but that's gone."

Collin walked over to the set of French doors that led to the side veranda and he looked out into the dusk. Then he glanced down at the door handles; even the handles were ornate and beautiful like everything else in their house.

"You have a really nice home," he said. "I never had a real home like everybody else has. They were all just temporary places. If it was some real awful place, you just had to suck it up until you got sent to the next one or you ran away. I always wondered how normal people lived in one place for years. I couldn't understand why I couldn't be in a real family with a real home. By the time I got to the Meckleys I couldn't do it." He turned back to Casey and Mike. "I don't care about having a real home any more. And I don't care about all those things that the other kids have. I don't. But I had a backpack. And did you see what they did to it? They cut it."

Casey got up and went over to his side.

"They couldn't help that, Collin. They had to do that to save your life."

"But what happened to it? And what happened to my hiking boots? And my book. That was my book. Mr. Everett gave it to me. What did they do with it?"

Without giving them a chance to answer, he continued.

"You asked me why I wanted to hike the Appalachian Trail. It's because of that book. I never even heard of the Appalachian Trail until like a month ago. The guy who wrote it did the whole trail and at the end of his hike he said that he had never felt so alive, so free, and so strong… And that's what I want.

"There's stuff all your researching wouldn't find out about me. Yeah, you'd see that my mom died when I was a baby and my dad disappeared when I was two, only to appear thirteen years later on the day before he was executed for killing some people. It would show the long list of homes and facilities where I was placed. But your research wouldn't show anything about me, about what I like or what I want."

He returned to the chair near the fireplace and sank down into it, staring at the flames.

"How many people do you know who grew up like I did? What kind of a life do you think this is? It's not a life. It might be an existence, but it's not living. I'm tired of just existing. I want to live. Who was it who said I have not yet begun to fight? John Paul

Jones? Well, for me, it's I have not yet begun to live. And I want to live. I want to feel alive. And I don't know how to make that happen..." He took a deep breath and for a moment he was silent, then he added, "But if that guy could feel that way by hiking the Appalachian Trail, then that's what I want to do and nobody is going to stop me."

For a moment the two lawyers who made their living by talking could not speak.

"I'm really tired," Collin said. "Can I go to sleep now?"

"Sure," said Casey. "There's a new toothbrush in your restroom and some sweatpants and tops in the top drawer of the bureau. If you want to take a shower now or in the morning, we can tape a plastic bag over your cast."

"In the morning," he said.

"Collin," Mike began, before he left the room. "I'll send out some inquiries tonight. We'll try and find what happened to your things, your book and hiking boots and do everything possible to get them back."

"Thanks," he said. He looked up at Casey and Mike. "I never did that before."

"What?" Casey asked.

"I never told anyone anything about myself. But you acted like you wanted to know and you acted like you cared."

"We did want to know," said Casey. "And we do care."

"Yes," Mike agreed. "And not just because we are your lawyers."

"You look exhausted, Collin," Casey said to him. "I hope you get some good rest tonight. Stay in bed as long as you want tomorrow, okay?"

“Okay,” he said.

After he left the room, both Mike and Casey went to work.

Chapter 8

The video of Collin being struck was played thousands of times in the weeks that followed the accident. The public was demanding that the cold-hearted and compassionless girl responsible for it should be held accountable.

A month after the accident, a hearing was held. Brooke Setree and her counsel sat on one side of the courtroom. Collin Talley sat on the other side with his lawyers.

Before either side could present their case, the judge spoke up, asking Brooke and Collin to approach the bench.

"This is a highly unusual case," said the judge. "On my left is a young man who doesn't much care about school or rules, on my right is a young lady who doesn't much care about anything or anybody. Did either one of you ever hear the statement 'let the punishment fit the crime'?"

He paused a moment staring at the two in front of him.

"When young people such as yourselves come before me, I see to it that the sentence I hand down is appropriate for the crime that was committed. For example, one seventeen year old girl had a habit of shoplifting. I sentenced her to wash and iron clothing at the women's emergency shelter every Saturday for one year. When a young man was caught stealing cars, he was sentenced to wash cars every weekend for one year and donate his pay to the local food bank. Now what would be an appropriate sentence for two young people with little regard for the people around them?"

He was silent for a moment, tapping his fingers.

"Perhaps the two of you need to spend a good amount of time together."

"No," said Brooke, as she looked over at Collin with disgust.

"Silence, young lady," the judge yelled.

Then he paused and looked at Collin.

"You wanted to hike, is that correct?"

Collin thought it was a trick question, but he answered.

"Yes."

"Then you will hike."

Collin held his breath. He didn't trust this judge, like all the others he had ever encountered in his life.

"Walking is a great physical and mental activity," the judge continued. "It has many therapeutic benefits. Yes, you will hike."

The judge next looked at the girl.

"Miss Setree, do you like to hike?"

"Me? Hike? You've got to be kidding! Why do you think they invented cars?"

"I'll take that as a no," said the judge. "I was hoping you would say that. You will hike also, Miss Setree."

"Yeah, right," said Brooke.

"Watch what you say, young lady, or you will be held in contempt," the judge admonished her.

The judge looked through some papers before him, then continued talking.

"There are approximately 230 miles of the Appalachian Trail in Pennsylvania extending north and east from the Maryland border at Pen Mar Park to the New Jersey border at the Delaware Water Gap. It is reported to be the rockiest section of the whole trail. Your initial meeting was right on the Appalachian Trail along Pennsylvania Route 183 when Miss Setree went speeding with utter disregard for both the individual in her car and everyone else around her. Miss Setree then carelessly struck Mr. Talley and with depraved indifference left the scene of the accident.

"After much deliberation, and keeping in mind that you two, no pun intended, ran into each other at an Appalachian Trail road crossing, it is the decision of this court to sentence you, Mr. Collin Talley, and you, Miss Brooke Sierra Setree, to walk together the length of the Appalachian Trail in Pennsylvania from the Maryland border to the New Jersey border."

"What?" Collin asked aloud. "I am not going to hike with her. There is no way I want to spend even one second with her."

"That is understandable," said the judge. "Contemptible creature that she is. You may find a rattlesnake a more honorable companion."

"Well, I surely don't want to be around you," the girl said to Collin. Then she looked up at the judge. "You've gotta be joking. I have no intention of walking anywhere. I don't walk. And I don't hike. That's the most stupid thing I have ever heard. I'm not going to do it, especially with that." She pointed to Collin.

The judge banged his gavel.

"Unless either one of you want to be held in contempt, you will not say another word."

Brooke turned and stared back at her lawyers and mouthed to them the words, "Do something!"

"You will start as soon as school is finished in June," said the judge, "as long as you, Mr. Talley, are sufficiently healed to do it and are given a clean bill of health from your doctors. Furthermore, you will start it together in Maryland, you will stay together and you will finish it together in New Jersey. You will sign in at all shelter registers and I will see you both when you have completed your sentence. Furthermore, you will not bring or use any cellphone, smartphone, two-way radio, walkie-talkie or any kind of electronic communication device. Is that understood?"

He banged the gavel and left the room.

"I'm not doing it with her," said Collin to his lawyers. "He can't make me."

"He must be out of his mind!" said Brooke quickly dialing her cell phone. "You're fired," she screamed to her lawyers. "Get out of my sight."

Then she looked at Collin.

"This is your fault," she said.

"Yeah, like I wanted you to take your car and slam it into my face."

"Don't worry," said the girl. "Your face will be just fine. You have the finest plastic surgeons that my parents' money can buy and besides it's a way bigger improvement than what it was. Don't even think for one second that I'm going anywhere with you."

"And I would rather be dead than have to be in your company for even a second," Collin shot back.

Chapter 9

There was nothing either of them could say or do about their sentence. The law had spoken and on the first Monday after the last day of school in June, Collin's lawyers dropped him off at Pen Mar Park on the Pennsylvania and Maryland border.

Even though the juvenile court proceedings were sealed, Brooke made everything known to the world about what that judge was making her do. The news media was there to record the start of their sentence. The World At Large news crew was there. And all of the rest of the paparazzi stood in a roped off area guarded by the local police. This was the closest the photographers would be allowed to come for the judge had issued an injunction preventing any of them from coming within a thousand feet of Collin and Brooke while they were carrying out their sentence.

Collin looked through the crowd but saw no sign of Brooke.

"Think she'll come?" Collin asked Casey Dare.

"She better," said Casey.

"Oh, good grief, here comes her entourage now," said Mike.

Three limos pulled up into the parking area.

Brooke stepped out of one of the limos wearing high heels, a short skirt and a sleeveless top. She took one look at Collin and turned up her nose.

"Where does she think she's going?" Collin asked. "To the mall?"

"Don't worry about her," said a familiar voice behind Collin. He turned and saw Curtis Everett, his English teacher from Nebraska, standing behind him.

"Mr. Everett," Collin said. "You're here."

The teacher nodded.

"I should be the one saying that," said Everett. "*You're here*. You're on the trail of trails."

"Yeah, but I never thought it would be like this," said Collin, looking over at Brooke. "And it was my dream to start at Springer, not in the middle."

"But you're here," said Everett. "And on the trail, anything can happen."

"Yeah," said Collin. "I guess."

"Do you still have the book I gave you?"

"Yeah, it was lost, but Casey and Mike got it back for me. It's in my pack."

"Good," said Everett. "I'm sure it's going to be a very interesting three weeks or so for both of you. I have something else for you."

The teacher handed him the guidebook and a set of the Appalachian Trail maps for the state of Pennsylvania.

"Awesome," said Collin.

"There's a lot of good information in this book," said Everett.

"Thanks, I don't know what to say…"

Everett patted him on his shoulder.

They turned when they heard noise from the second limo. Senator John Gordon Setree was engaged in an animated phone call. From the third limo came Mrs. Setree. She too had a cell phone in hand and ended the call the same time as her husband.

Mrs. Setree took a look at Collin and stared at him up and down.

"Did you pack your pepper spray?" she called to her daughter.

"Yes, mother."

The Senator walked over to Collin. He smiled for the cameras, but his words to Collin were brusque.

"Nothing better happen to my daughter out there. Do you hear me?"

"Don't worry," said Collin. "I'll keep an eye out at every road crossing to make sure she doesn't get hit by some crazy, speeding, reckless driver."

The judge as well drove up to see them off. He pulled Collin aside and said a few brief last words to him before his attention was focused on Brooke. He watched as Brooke looked through several pieces of luggage.

"What are you doing?" the judge asked her.

"I'm making sure everything is here. What else did you think I'd be doing?"

"You're going hiking," he said. "Where do you think you are going? To a luxury resort?"

"C'mon," said Collin to the girl angrily. "At the rate you're going, we're not going to get to the Antietam Shelter. We won't even make it to the Deer Lick Shelters by dark."

The girl looked over at the judge.

"And you said we weren't going to a luxury resort," she said shaking her head and rolling her eyes. "Antietam Shelter… Deer Lick Shelters… So they might have quaint names, but they're shelters. Just because they'll be in the woods, rustic doesn't mean they can't offer totally comfy accommodations."

She could see the judge was still confused about her opinion on the shelters so she explained it further for him.

"You see, my mother dragged me to all those shelters that her women's groups raised money for, and, believe me, those shelters are as plush as many of the hotels I've been in. So I am all set for this walking thing."

Collin shook his head. Was she going to be in for a surprise!

Everyone watched as Brooke had her driver put everything back in the limo and told him she would meet him later that day at the first hiker hotel.

"I'm ready now," she said, swinging her purse over her shoulder. "Which way do we go?"

"Aren't you bringing anything?" Collin asked her.

"Duh," she said, opening her little purse. "I have my lip gloss, my compact, my charge card, my smartphone and my little canister of pepper spray if you try anything stupid. What more do I need?"

Immediately the judge had her phone confiscated.

"Well," Collin began slowly. "I was thinking something more along the lines of say… hhmmm…water... and I don't know… let's say maybe a pair of… say… hiking boots."

"I'm not thirsty," she said. "And boots? Those big ugly things? They would make my feet look huge! No, I don't think so."

"Okay, that's it then. We should get going," Collin said as he picked up his pack. He said good-bye to his lawyers and the judge and his teacher.

"Let me take your picture," said Curtis Everett.

Even though he wasn't happy, Collin smiled for the camera, for he was about to take his first steps on the Appalachian Trail. It would have been a perfect start except for that girl.

"Take care, Collin," Curtis said, shaking his hand. "And good luck. I think, with her, you're really going to need it."

"Thanks, Mr. Everett."

Collin started, but held back a moment waiting for Brooke.

"Are you coming?" he called to her.

"Bye Mummy," Brooke said, brushing her cheek beside her mother's. "Good-bye, Father. I still don't understand why you couldn't have gotten a better lawyer to get me out of this."

"Believe me, I tried, darling," he said to her.

"See you soon," said Brooke, who then posed another five minutes for the cameras as if she was on the red carpet.

Collin watched her from a distance. She was unbelievable.

Brooke looked to see where Collin was and then headed in his direction.

When they were out of sight, Mrs. Setree entered her limo and drove away. Senator Setree went over to the judge who was standing next to Casey and Mike Dare.

"This was the best idea I ever had," the judge said to the Senator.

"But it was their idea," the Senator said pointing to Casey and Mike.

"That's hearsay," the judge smiled. "And I would object, but I didn't bring my gavel."

"Do you think my daughter will be safe out there with that boy?" the Senator asked the judge and the two lawyers.

"It is the boy that I would be more concerned about than that daughter of yours," said the judge.

"Yes, perhaps you are right," the Senator

regretfully agreed. “I hope this works. I don’t know what else to do. She is so out of control. It would be a different thing if we weren’t always under the country’s microscope.”

“One of the hazards of the political profession, my friend. You know, John, if that boy does survive this with her, you will owe him a great deal.”

“Yes, I will,” said the Senator. “I do have a concern. I have closed my daughter’s charge account like you had suggested. How will she ever get along without money and some proper hiking gear?”

“There’s this thing called trail magic,” said the judge. “There will be people along the way to make sure she has what she needs.”

Chapter 10

They began their trail journey, Collin up ahead, Brooke far behind.

Collin paused at the sign in front of him which read *Appalachian Trail to Maine: 1080 miles* with an arrow pointing to the right. Below this was a sign that read *Appalachian Trail to Georgia: 920 miles* and had an arrow pointing left. But it was the panoramic view just behind the sign that caught his eye. A large valley was in front of him and a distant blue ridge was on the horizon.

"So you decided to wait," she said rudely as she came up behind him.

"I didn't stop for you," Collin told her.

"Then why did you stop?"

He stared at her a long time. Not once did she glance at the awesome view of the wide-open valley dotted with farms and fields and distant hills. She didn't even see what was right in front of her. Finally, he shook his head and moved on.

"Say, how come we can't go this way?" she asked, motioning in the opposite direction.

"Because, brainless, New Jersey is this way."

"Don't call me that," she said angrily. "What makes you so sure the trail goes that way and not this way? Were you ever here before?"

"No."

"Well, then, what makes you the authority on this? How would you know the way to go?"

"Come here," he said.

She walked up to him, taking dainty small steps in her high heel shoes.

"See that white mark over there?" he said, pointing to a two inch by six inch white-painted rectangular mark on a tree up ahead. "That's called a blaze. We're going to follow those blazes. That's how it works on this trail."

"How far do we follow them?"

"Well, if you weren't with me, I could follow them all the way to Maine. But since you are with me, we will be following them to New Jersey."

He continued onward. His walking was easy, even though he carried a large pack on his back. His hiking boots felt fine. He turned to look and see how the girl was doing in her high heels. She was going so slow. There was no way she would be able to keep up with him.

"You were stupid to wear those shoes," he called to her.

"They match my purse."

"And that's another stupid thing. Carrying a purse but no water."

"Quit calling me stupid."

"We have to go faster than this if we want to make the first shelter by dark."

"How far is that?" she asked him.

"About five miles."

"Five miles!" she gasped in anger. "And we have to walk the whole way? When are we taking a break?"

"A break? We're not taking any breaks. We just got started."

They crossed railroad tracks, entered a wooded area and came to the sign that said *Mason-Dixon Line*.

"We are in Pennsylvania now," said Collin to the girl, glaring at her. "I sure hope we make it to the New Jersey border sometime before the next century. And I hope I make it there in one piece."

"Well, if you don't, it won't be any fault of mine."

"That's right," said Collin. "As long as you keep your distance, I'll be fine."

He turned and picked up his pace.

"Why must you go so fast?" she called to him.

"Why must you go so slow?" he said to her.

It took forever for them to reach the bridge that crossed Falls Creek, a distance of not even a mile from where they had started. Brooke took off her shoes and walked in the water.

"This feels great," she said.

"C'mon," he said. "Quit playing around. We gotta get up Mount Dunlop."

"Nobody said anything about a mountain," she said, putting her high heels back on.

"It's only about 1400 or 1500 feet."

"We have to climb that high?" she asked. "I thought there was a law against cruel and unusual punishment." She reached for her phone and realized it was not there. "What am I going to do?" she cried.

"You're going to stop acting like a baby and hike. We are already at about 1000 feet. The climb up is only going to be about five hundred feet, so it's no big deal."

He started going at his pace and soon left her behind. When he reached the crest he sat down and waited.

And waited. It was an interminable wait, so he stood and began walking further ahead.

She looked up the trail. Collin was nowhere in sight.

"Hey," she called out to him. "Where are you?"

She inched her way along and heard something up ahead. Perhaps Collin was coming back. But it wasn't Collin. There was a man with a red bandanna on his head coming towards her at a fast pace. His clothes hung loosely on him and he was wearing a pack smaller than Collin's.

"Hey, how are you doing?" he called to her.

She didn't answer him but quickly pulled her pepper spray out of her purse.

"Stay back," she said. "I know how to use this."

He put his hands up.

"Calm down, little lady," he said. "Your friend up ahead was right."

"My friend? What do you mean?"

"He warned me about you. He told me to beware of the Spoiled Little Princess. He was right. And here I thought that bears were the only thing I was going to be afraid of out here."

The hiker flashed her a smile and continued on his way south on the trail.

Brooke took a moment to look around. She was alone on the trail, surrounded by trees, creepy guys and who knows what else? Bears?

"And snakes," she said to herself in alarm.

She tried to walk a little faster, but it was hard in high heels.

There was a noise behind her and she turned.

A girl wearing a pack the same size as Collin's was racing towards her.

"Hey, wait up," the girl called to Brooke.

"What do you want?" Brooke asked, eyeing her warily.

"Are you the Spoiled Little Princess?"

"What?" Brooke asked angrily. "Not only are you rude, but you smell."

"Oh, awesome," said the girl smiling and extending her hand. "I'm Tennessee Tara."

Brooke did not take the girl's hand.

The girl smiled.

"Of course, you wouldn't shake my hand. You've gotta live up to that trail name. How far are you going?"

"Not that it's any of your business," said Brooke, "but some gap near New Jersey."

"The Delaware Water Gap? And you are seriously doing it in high heels? I would never have believed it if I hadn't seen it with my own eyes. Wow, that is so cool."

"It's not cool," said Brooke, snidely. "And I don't want to be here. If it wasn't for that juvenile delinquent…"

"What juvenile delinquent?" Tennessee Tara asked her.

"That juvenile delinquent up ahead of me."

Tennessee Tara thought quietly for a moment before speaking.

"The Spoiled Little Princess and the Juvenile Delinquent," Tennessee Tara said slowly. And then she repeated it. "The Spoiled Little Princess and the Juvenile Delinquent. I love it. Those are just about the best names I came across yet."

"Are you crazy?" Brooke yelled in indignation. "My name is Brooke."

"No," said Tennessee Tara with a smile on her face. "You're the Spoiled Little Princess. I'm stopping at the Deer Lick Shelters tonight. If you're going to be there, the mac and cheese are on me."

Brooke watched as the girl went speeding up the trail. Her legs were shaped as if she spent hours in the gym.

"Hey," Brooke called to her. "Where do you work out at?"

"Right here," said Tennessee Tara pointing with both index fingers to the trail below her feet. "It's the best."

Brooke continued on at her slow pace and finally ran into Collin.

"Well, congratulations," Collin said to her. "You just walked two miles in two and a half hours."

"Thanks," she said proudly. "That *is* a pretty good pace."

"Yeah," said Collin. "For a sloth."

"Do me a favor and shut up."

They walked along in silence, Collin looking around at the trees, Brooke staring at the ground in front of her feet, watching every inch of the trail.

"Why did you tell those people I was a Spoiled Little Princess?"

"I thought you told me to shut up."

"Just answer the question."

"Well, it's what you are," said Collin. "And why did you tell Tennessee Tara I was the Juvenile Delinquent?"

"Because that's what you are," she glared at him. "It fits. See, I know all about you. And I know all about your father."

"You know all about my father?" Collin asked. "Then you probably know more about him than I do. He left when I was two."

"Oh," said Brooke.

"So maybe you don't know me at all."

"Maybe, I don't."

Everything she knew about him was from what she had heard from her parents talking to her lawyers. He was a truant and runaway from somewhere out west and the son of a convicted and executed murderer. Surely he was following in his father's footsteps. She couldn't be wrong about something like that. Her instincts never let her down before. And yet something about him made her pause, but she didn't know why. She turned away from him. He was not like any other boy she knew.

Again Collin pulled away from her, but slowed every so often, waiting for Brooke to catch up.

"Say, how did that Tennessee girl know to call me that awful name?" she called to Collin. "She was coming from behind me. She hadn't passed by me, so how would she have known to call me that name?"

"There's an incredible system of communication out here," said Collin. "You don't need a phone to communicate. See, I had talked to Just Harry, a southbound section hiker. He was that first guy we saw wearing the red bandanna. He passed us, heading south on the trail and he ran into Tennessee Tara, who was heading north. People share information when they meet. And I guess it's not every day that someone is out on the trail carrying…" he stopped and started laughing. "…a purse and hiking in high heel shoes."

"Stop laughing," she said.

But he couldn't stop. He sank to his knees laughing at her.

Full of anger she continued up the trail without him. She followed the blazes like he had told her and crossed a couple roads before continuing once again along the tree-lined trail.

She began to feel thirsty in the warmth of that June afternoon and was wondering if she should have brought a little bottle of spring water. Then she saw the sign for Bailey's Spring and she went to it and took a little sip. She didn't know if it was safe to drink without filtering it, but she was so thirsty, she didn't care. She was not carrying any type of filter or water purifier like real long distance hikers carried.

She walked on, but turned back looking for Collin. It was too creepy being out in the woods all alone. Maybe she should wait for him. Maybe she went the wrong way. But she looked up and saw the small rectangular white blazes on trees up ahead of her, so she knew she was going the right way. She wondered how much farther it was till the shelter.

She soon heard people talking behind her and she looked back to see Collin with two hikers.

"That's her," said Collin.

"With those shoes I'd know her anywhere," said the first hiker.

The first hiker approached her and stopped a foot away to look at her.

"Wow," he said. "It's true."

"All right," she said. "Laugh it up. I heard it all before."

"We heard all about you," said the first hiker. "Hello Spoiled Little Princess, I'm the Rock Man and I am happy to meet you."

"Listen, Rockhead," she began. "Don't call me Spoiled Little Princess."

"Fine," he said. "But can I take your picture?"

"No, you may not!"

"Hi," said the other hiker. "They call me Southern Cross."

"Just how many of you are out here?" Brooke asked.

"Well let's see," Southern Cross began. "Last I heard 1,800 had passed through Neel's Gap."

"What?" Brooke gasped. "There's eighteen hundred of you out here?"

"I don't know how long ago that amount was posted," said Southern Cross, "but I'm sure it's a lot more than that now. Then you got your section hikers, your flip-flop hikers, your weekend hikers and you always have day hikers out and then of course the southbounders will be coming."

"Of course," said Brooke. "The southbounders. Can't forget them." Whatever the heck was he talking about? "So, what did *you* do that they made you come out here?"

"Come again?" said Rock Man.

"What did you do that they made you come out here? Rob a bank?"

"Princess, nobody but me made me come out here."

"Then, are you out of your mind? Why would any sane person want to be out here? There are bugs and it's hot and, say, where's the nearest bathroom around here?"

She looked around and saw nothing but trees, trees in every direction as far as the eye could see.

"First of all we are outdoors, not indoors. Therefore, there's no indoor plumbing here," said Southern Cross.

A look of horror washed over her face.

"This isn't fair," she said. "What am I supposed to do?"

Southern Cross and Rock Man looked at Collin.

"Didn't your girlfriend ever go camping before?"

"That's disgusting," said Collin. "She's not my girlfriend."

"I wouldn't be here," Brooke screamed, "if it wasn't for that lousy judge saying we were supposed to do this hike together."

"The judge…?" Southern Cross asked.

"Yeah," said Collin. "This is our sentence. To hike the A.T. from Pen Mar to the Delaware Water Gap together. The only thing we have in common is that we hate each other."

"Awesome," Southern Cross laughed.

"This is just too cool," said Rock Man raising his hand to high five his friend's hand.

"It is not cool," said Brooke. "I have to go to the bathroom and there are no bathrooms in sight."

"Look," said Southern Cross. "Whatever you do indoors, you can do it outdoors."

"What? I am not going to the bathroom out here! Not when there's weirdos like you around."

"You have to," said the Rock Man. "It's no big deal."

"Maybe to you it isn't."

"Look, you're not the only girl out here in the woods. What do you think Tennessee Tara does?" Southern Cross asked Brooke. "All you have to do is look for a bunch of trees, a rhododendron patch, pine trees, whatever, and you have all the privacy you need. Really, it's no big deal. But just make sure you watch out for poison ivy. It has three leaves. And you definitely don't want to get poison on you."

Southern Cross motioned to Rock Man that they should head up the trail.

"Maybe we'll see you up at the shelter," Rock Man said to Brooke and Collin.

"Don't count on it," said Collin. "If we're lucky we might make it there by next week."

Collin watched as the two thru-hikers took off and when they disappeared up the trail, he turned and looked at Brooke. She was looking off into the woods.

Somebody will see me, Brooke thought to herself. She looked up and saw Collin staring at her.

"What are you staring at?" she growled to him.

"Nothing. I'll be up ahead."

She took one step off the trail and then another, looking up in every direction as far as she could see, searching to see if anyone was there. There was no one in sight. But she couldn't do it.

Collin stood waiting for her further up the trail, his back to her. He turned when he heard her coming.

"Well?" he said to her.

"Well, what?"

"You didn't go, did you?"

"It's none of your business," she yelled.

"No, you didn't go," he said, knowing she wouldn't. "Well, you better get used to it."

"I can't go to the bathroom out here. There's too many people out here."

Collin looked up and down the trail and at all the trees that surrounded them. There was no one in sight.

"Well," she said, looking around as he was doing. "Maybe not at this moment, but someone could be coming by at any time."

"Suit yourself," said Collin walking on.

For the next hour they saw no one. Collin pulled further and further ahead of Brooke.

Brooke kept looking into the trees, trying to find a suitable place to take a break. Just when she thought she had found the perfect place, she changed her mind. She couldn't go to the bathroom out here in the open.

This was the cruelest thing that had ever happened in her whole life. She couldn't believe that her mother and father, as important and powerful as they were, could not have prevented her from having to do this barbaric and brutal punishment.

A tear fell from her face. Her feet hurt, she was thirsty and she had to go to the bathroom.

"Awww, what's wrong, Princess?" Collin asked her mockingly, as he waited for her by the side of the trail.

"Somebody will pay for this," she said.

"Can't you enjoy being out here in the trees and sunshine?"

"I don't like trees."

"Can't you enjoy these awesome thru-hikers passing us?" he said as he started walking beside her at her slow pace. "They come from all over America and all around the world."

"No. There are some really weird people out here. They are so disgusting and dirty and poor."

"Why do you think they're poor? And what's wrong with being poor?"

"If they had money they wouldn't be out here."

Collin stopped walking and faced her.

"You have money and you're out here. And where do you get your strange ideas from? Do you know why Rock Man is called the Rock Man?"

"No."

"He just got his Ph.D. in geology. He's writing a book about the geology of the Appalachian Trail. And Southern Cross is a computer geek from California who made his first million when he was twenty and sailed around the world on his own yacht when he turned twenty-one."

"A millionaire with his own yacht? Then, I don't understand why they're doing this if they don't have to."

"You just don't get it," said Collin, annoyed by her condescending attitude.

"Don't use that tone with me. Why don't you just leave me alone?"

So he did. He pulled ahead of her and disappeared up the trail.

"Go ahead," she said in a voice only she could hear. "Keep right on going."

She needed to be by herself. She needed to take a break long before she could make it to the shelter. Searching the trees, she found a nice thicket with plenty of privacy. She glanced up the trail and down. There was no one there, but for another five minutes she studied the surrounding woods, listening and wondering if someone was out there, perhaps with a camera. Finally, she felt no one was nearby and she entered the trees, quickly did what she had to do, and walked back to the trail, watching the entire time to see if anyone had seen her leave the trail and get back on it. No one had. No one was there.

She started walking and up ahead she saw the back of Collin as he slowly made his way north.

"You okay?" he asked, sounding for a moment like he was genuinely concerned about her.

"Of course," she said arrogantly.

For a moment he was concerned about her, but as soon as she opened her mouth and Collin heard her caustic tone, he realized his mistake.

"Someone will pay for this," she said angrily. "If it's the last thing I do…"

“Hey, Spoiled Little Princess,” said Collin. “You keep whining like that and they’ll give you the name Cry Baby.”

“I mean it,” said the girl. “Someone will pay for this. This is the worst thing that could have possibly happened to me. When my father becomes the president, I’ll see that that judge gets fired for what he did.”

Chapter 11

"Owww," Brooke cried, her steps getting smaller and smaller and her pace getting slower and slower. Her feet were in constant pain from blisters from her high heels.

"Why don't you take those stupid shoes off and walk barefoot?" Collin asked her.

"They're not stupid shoes," she said. "I paid twelve hundred dollars for these. I didn't think it was going to be like this. I didn't know we were going up and down these awful hills and constantly stepping over stones and tree roots. How could you possibly think I would walk barefoot over these rocks?"

"I have to tell you," Collin started. "You have the perfect trail name. You look like a Spoiled Little Princess. You act like a Spoiled Little Princess. You sound like a Spoiled Little Princess. You *are* a Spoiled Little Princess. It's the most incredibly perfect trail name for you."

"The perfect what?"

"Trail name," said Collin. "All thru-hikers have trail names out here. No one knows you by your real name, just your trail name."

"And the perfect name for you is Juvenile Delinquent."

"I don't want that for a trail name," said Collin.

"And just what should your trail name be?"

"I don't know," he said. "It must be something unique and special to the individual hiker. I have to think about it yet, but it's not going to be Juvenile Delinquent."

"Then you better stop calling me Spoiled Little Princess."

"Maybe if you stop acting like one, I won't call you that. But I don't know how you could stop acting and being what you have been your whole life."

"Look, just go," she said, waving him away. "I don't want to talk to you any more."

By the time they made it to the Deer Lick Shelters, Brooke was hobbling on her bare feet. All the hikers that had passed them and a few others that had already been at the shelter stood around them in a semi-circle waiting and gave the two of them a round of applause when they came into the camp.

"Let's hear it for the Spoiled Little Princess and the Juvenile Delinquent."

Collin smiled at their humor, while Brooke glared at them in indignation.

"Hey, I got extra macaroni and cheese," said Tennessee Tara offering it to Brooke and Collin.

"I got some tape for your feet," said another hiker who knelt down by Brooke. "I'm not a doctor, but I did take a course in first aid and I think you have some serious blisters. If you want, I can take a look at your feet."

Brooke was tired, hungry, in pain and desperate. She nodded to the hiker who offered to tend to her feet.

"I have a pair of sandals," said Tennessee Tara. "You could use them until you get a pair of boots."

"So how much farther is it to the shelter?" Brooke asked the hikers gathered there.

"Which shelter?" Tennessee Tara asked.

"The first one we're supposed to come to... What's it called? The Deer Lick Shelter?"

"These are the Deer Lick Shelters," said Tennessee Tara.

Brooke shook her head staring at the twin lean-to log structures.

"No," said Brooke. "This isn't it. I did volunteer work at women's shelters and this is nothing like that. The kind of place I'm supposed to be staying at is a real shelter. They dropped off all my things there. That's the shelter I'm supposed to be at."

Some of the hikers started laughing.

"Listen, Princess," said one of the hikers. "Out here, this is the only kind of shelter there is. There isn't any other kind."

"Wait a minute," said Brooke. "There has to be. This isn't a shelter. I can't stay here. There are only three walls to these hovels. There is no door. There is no bathtub and there are no beds."

"That's your fault," said Collin as he took off his pack. "You should have carried some gear instead of that ridiculous purse."

"This is my favorite purse," said Brooke. "It matches these shoes."

"You're not carrying anything for her?" Tennessee Tara asked Collin.

"No, of course not," he said.

"You don't have anything with you?" Tennessee Tara asked Brooke.

"Look, I didn't think it was going to be like this," Brooke cried out. "How was I supposed to know?"

Tennessee Tara opened her pack and pulled out a windbreaker.

"You can have this," she said. "It's gets cool at night. You're going to need it."

"I don't wear used clothing," said Brooke, indignantly. "Even if it was clean, which it isn't."

"Well, if you get cold tonight, it's here if you want it. I made macaroni and cheese if you'd like some."

Brooke turned up her nose.

"I hate macaroni and cheese," said Brooke.

"Perhaps her majesty would care to see the menu," said Collin.

They were all laughing at her.

This was so totally not fair, Brooke thought to herself. She glared at Collin and watched as he set up a little stove. He poured water into a little pan and when it boiled, he dumped in a pouch of powdered cheese and potatoes.

Brooke watched as the potatoes cooked and she felt faint from hunger.

"I'll give you one hundred dollars for those," Brooke said to Collin.

Collin put his hand out.

"I don't have it on me, stupid," she said.

"Then you can't have any," he told her.

"When we get back, I swear I'll give you the money."

"Nah, I don't want your money."

"I'll give you five hundred dollars," she continued.

"No."

"A thousand," she said.

"For a thousand, I would do it. But I don't trust you and I think when we did get back, you would not give me the money. So, no deal."

The potatoes finished cooking and Collin tasted them.

"Wow, are these good!" he exclaimed loudly.

"Stop it," she said. "How can you be so cruel?"

"Cruel?" he said. He stared at her, his eyes burning into her. "Cruel? Cruel is lying face down in the road in pain and being unable to breathe and unable to move and having the person who did it to you yell about the damage to her car while she doesn't care one bit about the person she hit. That's cruel."

There was silence.

"Wow," said one of the hikers to Brooke. "Is that what you did to him?"

But Brooke didn't answer him. She looked away and said nothing.

For the rest of the night no one said anything to Brooke. She avoided them and they avoided her.

She sat up the entire night, shivering, not taking the windbreaker Tennessee Tara had left out for her.

Near dawn she curled up near a log and in exhaustion fell asleep.

"What are you going to do with her?" Tennessee Tara asked Collin as they looked at the sleeping Brooke in the early morning light.

"I have no idea," said Collin. "She's incredible, self-centered, spoiled… I don't know. It might take us six months to get Pennsylvania done, the same amount of time it would take everyone else to do the whole entire two thousand miles."

"Good luck," Tennessee Tara said patting him on the back. "Let me know how you make out."

Near noon Brooke stirred. She reached for her purse and took out her compact. Her face was dirty. How could she put make-up on over her dirty face? Her hair was a mess and she had never felt this hungry and dirty and tired.

"I feel dizzy," she said to Collin. "I'm hungry."

"Check that bag hanging from that ceiling log," he motioned to her. "There might be something in it."

She reached up and took down a bag someone had left suspended on the mouse-proof rope. Inside it she found an apple and a pack of crackers. She ripped open the crackers and stuffed them into her mouth. Then she did the same with the apple.

"You didn't sign the register," he said to her, handing her a notebook and pen.

"What am I supposed to write in here?"

"Sign your name and put the date. Write a message if you want."

She took the pen and began to write.

I have died and gone to hell, she wrote. *Somebody wake me up from this nightmare or better yet come and save me.* She stared at her words then signed her name. *Brooke*.

Then she saw Collin's entry above hers.

The day is full of sunshine. Pennsylvania is incredibly pretty. I have never seen trees looking so incredibly green. The leaves reflecting the sunshine look like gold. I am happy to have started my first steps on the Appalachian Trail. I liked the view of the valley I saw when I first entered Pen Mar Park. When I saw the Mason-Dixon line I knew it was only the beginning of this some two hundred and thirty mile journey. I just hope the Spoiled Little Princess won't spoil everything with her cry baby attitude. Collin Talley a.k.a. The Juvenile Delinquent.

"I thought you said you didn't like your… what do you call it? Your trail name?"

"I changed my mind," said Collin. "Besides, all the thru-hikers think it's cool. And if they think it's cool, it must be so. You ready to head out, now?"

Resignedly she got to her feet. The sandals were still there that Tennessee Tara had given her. Carrying her shoes in one hand, she reluctantly slipped on the sandals and yelled, "Gross!"

She began walking. The sandals were not uncomfortable and she was not in pain like she had been with her high heels.

In just a couple miles they came to the Antietam Shelter. While Collin signed the register, Brooke soaked her feet in the Antietam Creek.

"Brooke!" someone yelled.

Brooke looked up. Her friend Laura was there.

"Laura!"

Laura gasped as she saw Brooke with her feet in the creek. "Is that you? You look terrible. What did he do to you?"

Laura glared at Collin.

"Oh, Laura," Brooke sighed. "I can't do this. Where's your car?"

"It's right over there in that little parking lot near those picnic tables. I'm sure glad I found you. I wasn't sure if you had passed by or not, but I was planning on waiting here all day hoping to see you."

"Just get me out of here, Laura."

Brooke leaned on Laura as they headed to the parking lot.

Collin followed them. As they got in the car, Collin reached over past Brooke in the passenger seat and took the keys out of the ignition.

"Hey, stop," Laura yelled. "What are you doing?"

"Get out of the car," Collin said to Brooke, his face inches from hers. His voice was deadly serious. "We're doing this. I don't care if you have to crawl." He looked at Laura. "You can't interfere with this. If you want to help her, get her a pair of boots, a backpack, a sleeping bag, food and a water bottle. But you're not going to make her get off the trail only seven miles after starting." He looked back at Brooke. "You'll be going back to your castle, Princess, but they'll be putting me back in the dungeon and I'm not going to let you do that to me."

For a moment no one said a word then Laura looked at Brooke.

"You walked seven miles?" Laura gasped. "Brooke, that's awesome."

"We only went seven miles?" Brooke sighed. "It feels like we did at least thirty or forty."

For a moment Laura studied Collin's face. She could see the fear and helplessness in his eyes, but she felt his resolve and heard the determination in his voice. Then she saw the trace of the scars above and below his left eye and she had a flashback to what she had seen on the news: Brooke's car striking him, Collin flying through the air and lying hurt and still in the road and Brooke screaming about her car. If anything, Brooke owed it to him to continue the hike for what she did to him.

"Maybe he's right," said Laura looking back at Brooke. "Maybe you just need the right gear and maybe you gotta keep going and finish this thing."

"Maybe you better take my side on this," Brooke said angrily to Laura, "if you want to still be my friend."

Laura reached into her glove compartment and popped the trunk.

"I brought you some things," said Laura getting out of the car. "I know you shouldn't have gone on a hike with nothing but your purse."

She pulled out a backpack.

"I didn't know what all to bring, but you should be able to find about everything you need in here."

"Oh, thanks so much, good friend," said Brooke sarcastically.

Laura struggled to lift it out of the trunk.

"It's pretty heavy, but the sales clerk made sure you have everything you need."

"Thanks a lot," said Brooke. "How am I supposed to lift this, much less carry it?"

Laura shrugged.

"I don't know, Brooke, but there's also a pair of boots here. I tried them on and they fit pretty good. Since we have the same size feet, I knew they would be a perfect fit for you."

Brooke looked at the boots in disgust.

"Just leave everything here and go," said Brooke hatefully.

Laura stared at her friend.

"Brooke, I'm just trying to help…"

"Go ahead," said Brooke angrily. "Leave."

Laura looked at Collin and he handed her the keys.

"I won't forget this," Brooke said to her angrily.

Laura drove away and Brooke tore through the pack looking for something to eat.

There was a bag of chocolate candy and nuts and a jar of peanut butter and packs of plain crackers. There were bagels and pita bread and packets of tuna. There were assorted pouches of food that could be mixed with boiling water for a hot meal. There were two two-liter bottles of water and a pump to sterilize water from the springs on the trail. There was a little stove, fuel, a spoon and a tiny pan. There were socks and a pair of boots, which she painfully and slowly put on. She found two pair of short hiking pants and one pair of long pants for sleeping or to wear if it was too cool to hike in shorts. She found two tops, a baseball hat, a bandanna, a long sleeve jacket, a plastic rain poncho and a little headlight. Inside a small designer bag, she found toiletries and quickly opened a packet of moistened towelettes to use on her hands and face.

"Next stop is the Tumbling Run Shelter," Collin said to her.

"I don't care," Brooke said to him. "Just go."

"Are you coming?"

"Of course," she said in resignation. "Where else would I be going?"

Even with the hiking boots, the pace was still horrendously slow. Thru-hikers passed by them like Collin and Brooke were standing still.

They signed in at the Tumbling Run Shelter and headed uphill.

"I'm checking this out," Collin called to Brooke when he saw a sign that said *Chimney Rocks*. "Are you coming?"

"No," she said.

He climbed up the rocky outcropping and sat down to stare out at the green hills. Brooke was missing the view like usual, he thought to himself. When he was done checking it out, he climbed back down off the boulders.

Brooke was waiting for him at the sign. She felt no need to walk any extra steps just to see a view.

"How far must we go yet?" she asked.

"We have another two miles to go until we get to the power line."

"Only two miles?"

"Yes."

In forty minutes they reached the power line cut.

"So where is the shelter?" Brooke asked when they got there.

"We didn't get there yet."

"You said we had another two miles to go."

"Yeah, to the power line. We still have around three miles or so until we reach the shelter."

"You're trying to trick me."

"No," he said. "I was trying to see if you were listening."

The trail began going downhill.

"Did I tell you how boring I think this is?" she said to him.

"Boring is a flat, open land with no mountains and no forests. Try living there and come back here. You will never say this is boring again."

They walked on in silence until they had walked a long ten-mile day and stopped for the night at the Rocky Mountain Shelters.

We did five miles yesterday and ten miles today, Collin wrote in the register. *That's progress. We're going to try for a thirteen mile stretch tomorrow to make it to the Birch Run Shelter. Hike on! Juvenile Delinquent.*

He handed the register to Brooke.

This is torture, not progress, she wrote. *Every time you get to a downhill, you find out you must immediately go up an extraordinarily steep uphill. Brooke.*

She looked over at Collin.

"Don't you think thirteen miles is a bit much?" she asked him. "Why can't we just rest and stay here tomorrow?"

"No," he said. "Thirteen miles is not too much unless you're a whiny cry baby princess."

"And just how many mountains will we have to climb tomorrow?"

He pulled out his map.

"Let's see. Good news, your majesty. It's all downhill to Caledonia State Park."

"Let me see that map," she said.

She took it from his hands and studied the elevation profile.

"Sure it's downhill to Caledonia State Park," she said. "But it's all uphill after that, you little liar."

"I wasn't lying. It *is* all downhill to Caledonia."

"Yeah, but it is all uphill after that. And you want to go all the way over here to the Birch Run Shelter? Why can't we just go to the Quarry Gap Shelter?"

"Because that's only about a seven mile hike. And we're not going to only do a seven mile day."

Early the next morning after they had hiked three miles, they came to a busy roadway.

"Route 30," Collin said to her. "Watch out for reckless drivers."

"Yeah, yeah. Why don't you give it a rest?"

"Nah. I can't do that."

Brooke looked at the long line of traffic in the road.

"Look at these lucky people living their normal lives," said Brooke.

Collin paused at the high volume of cars and trucks traveling on the highway as they waited for a break in the traffic. He had a flashback to when he would watch the cars from his place by the billboard back in Nebraska.

"Makes you wonder where they're all going," Collin said aloud.

"No, it doesn't make me wonder that at all. Who cares where they are going?"

"I was just wondering. Don't you ever wonder about things?"

"No, not about things like that. Do you know that you are different from anyone else I have ever met in my whole life?"

"Yeah, well, I've never met anyone like you either."

There was a break in the traffic and they ran across the road. For a short while the path was level and smooth as they walked past the campground's picnic pavilions in Caledonia State Park. They filled their water bottles at a park drinking fountain but once they were past the pavilions, they began climbing a steep hill.

Brooke stopped every so often to catch her breath and was happy when she finally reached the top.

"We're in Michaux State Forest," he said to her. "We've been in it since the first shelter."

"Like you really think I care what the name of this place is?"

They continued uphill and stopped at the Quarry Gap Shelter.

"This is a different kind of shelter," Collin said to a very disinterested Brooke.

He studied the structure. Two small shelters were linked together by a common roof. In the space between the two shelters was a roofed-in area in which the local trail maintaining club had provided a large picnic table for hikers to eat at.

Collin took the Quarry Gap Shelter register to the picnic table and signed in.

"Can't we stay here tonight?" Brooke asked him. "I'm tired."

"We didn't go that far today," he said. "Besides, the next shelter isn't that far."

"Not far? It's still a good seven miles to the Birch Run Shelter. Can't we take a break here?"

"Yeah, we'll eat lunch here and head out in twenty minutes."

It was more than half an hour before they started hiking again.

Collin liked all the different kinds of trees that were along the trail, even if he didn't know what they all were. Sometimes groves of oak. Sometimes there were thickets of mountain laurel. But they soon came to Collin's favorite kind of tree: the evergreen.

"This is really cool," said Collin. "Look, it's an alley of evergreens."

The trees lined both sides of the trail. He loved the strong pine fragrance that permeated the air and he stopped in front of a six-foot tree.

"This one would make a great Christmas tree," he said.

"That tiny thing? I don't think we ever had one smaller than twelve feet."

"A twelve foot tree? That's huge!" said Collin. "But I guess living in a castle, you must have some pretty high ceilings in that place."

"I don't live in a castle."

"Yeah, right."

Late in the day they came to a large opening in the trees and there sat the twin Birch Run Shelters.

Brooke was famished. She tore open the envelope of tuna and poured it into a pita pocket. She drank water and stuffed candy into her mouth. She then rolled out her sleeping bag and immediately fell fast asleep.

Chapter 12

As soon as Brooke awoke the next morning, she felt ill at ease. There was a heavy cold fog in the air. This was not a day to be outside, let alone in the middle of nowhere.

Other hikers who had come into the shelters late the night before were already heading out, disappearing into the fog.

"It's creepy," she said to herself and tried to roll deeper into her sleeping bag.

"C'mon wake up," said Collin, gently tapping her side with the toe of his boot.

"Stop it," she yelled angrily. "I'm not going anywhere until the sun comes up."

"Fine," said Collin. "But it's already after eight and I'm heading out now. Don't forget to sign the register."

He put the notebook by her side.

"I filled your water bottles, too."

"You touched my water bottles?" she said from the warmth of her sleeping bag. "I don't want your cooties on my stuff."

"Fine, I'll dump it out and you can go get your own water and purify it."

She opened one eye and watched him, but he didn't touch her water bottles. He just closed his own pack and hoisted it onto his back and she watched him head away from the shelter.

He was going ahead without her.

She sat up and climbed out of her sleeping bag. This was definitely not a day to be out in the woods. It was damp and miserable and visibility was no more than ten feet. In seconds Collin had disappeared and there was not another hiker in sight.

A chill ran up Brooke's back when she realized she was completely alone in the dismal cloud that covered the mountaintop. She quickly put on her long pants and jacket.

"Hey, wait up," she called to Collin. "I'm coming."

She threw on her boots and quickly stowed away her sleeping bag. She swallowed a handful of nuts and saw the trail register by her side.

The fog is overwhelming, she wrote. *It's creepy. The Spoiled Little Princess.*

"Boo," said a voice behind her.

It was Collin. He had tricked her by sneaking around the shelter and coming up behind her to scare her.

Brooke jumped and swung out her arm to hit him, but he was too quick for her and he jumped out of her way.

"Don't scare me," she said. "This is spooky enough without you adding to it."

Collin laughed.

"It's just fog. It will probably burn off by mid-morning."

"Then we should wait till then."

"Wait? No, Princess, I'm not waiting a few hours just because you're scared. C'mon. Let's go."

He headed away from the Birch Run Shelters and disappeared into the mist.

Brooke quickly picked up her pack. Again Collin was nowhere in sight. She walked into the oppressive fog. She did not like Collin, but as an overwhelming aloneness descended on her, she scrambled down the trail as quickly as she could, hoping she would catch a glimpse of him. Having him around was better than being totally alone in this wilderness.

"Hey," she called out to Collin. "Where are you? Hey, wait up."

She kept looking around wondering how far ahead he was. Hearing traffic up ahead, she kind of expected he would be waiting at the road crossing, but he wasn't.

She walked on for more than a mile, her anger building. Didn't the judge say they were supposed to be doing this together?

"Where are you, delinquent boy?" she yelled out.

There was no response, except a faint rustling in the trees off to her right.

She paused and listened. The noise stopped. When she continued walking, she heard it again.

Her eyes grew large as she glanced to her right and listened. Staring off into the fog, she tried to see who or what was making the noise. But she could see nothing.

The fog seemed to roll in even thicker as she continued walking and cast an eerie pall over the mountain. As she glanced up off to her right a sign caught her eye. It read: *Dead Woman's Hollow Road.*

What was that dreadful sign doing out here? It was more than just the chill and dampness in the air that made her shiver.

Even though the fog prevented her from seeing any distance, she looked up the trail as far as she could see. There was no sight of Collin. She looked behind her. There was no one. She was totally alone in the forest. But she heard the rustling again. It was closer now and she realized she wasn't all alone. There was someone out there.

It was just like the movies, she thought, a lone teen-age girl in the woods with a killer stalking her.

She reached for her pepper spray. The noise continued, but still she could not see anyone. Nor did she want to see the monster that was following her and making that rustling noise, taunting her when she was so scared to begin with. She had to get out of there.

Never mind, now, trying to see who it was; she knew who it was: some crazy lunatic who escaped from the mental asylum and was going to kill her.

She began running as fast as her pack would let her. Then realizing she would never make it with her pack on, she pulled it off and threw it down. She ran but kept glancing back to see if whoever, or whatever it was, was gaining on her.

She slipped on a pebble and slid off her feet, listening for the rustling behind her. Staring backwards, she slowly stood up with the little canister of pepper spray in her hand ready to use.

Just like in the movies, she knew that the killer would somehow automatically get in front of her. And he did. He was so close she could hear him breathing. Instinctively, her arm went up and at the very moment as she was turning and unleashing the pepper spray, she heard a voice.

"Hey, why are you running…"

The voice stopped as she turned to face her attacker and saw the spray going directly into Collin's face. He sank to the ground, screaming. His eyes were burning.

She froze as Collin collapsed, writhing in pain and holding his eyes.

“What did you do that for?” he cried out.

“Someone was out there,” she gasped. “They were chasing me...”

Beyond Collin’s cries, she heard the rustling again. It was very close, right by the side of the trail. As she turned, there it was… It was nothing more than a chipmunk scurrying around in the leaves. A chipmunk, a lousy little chipmunk making all that noise and scaring her like that.

“It was just a…” she began to say chipmunk, but stopped and looked at Collin.

The pepper spray had totally incapacitated her would-be attacker. She watched as Collin struggled to get his pack off, then blindly try to grasp his water bottle with one hand while the other hand was pressed up against his face. But the bottle dropped from his hand and rolled away. In exasperation and pain he cried out.

“No, no, no,” he yelled.

She slowly realized what she had done. She had hurt him. He was injured and they were all alone.

What am I going to do, she thought, thinking only of herself. She watched him struggling to reach his water bottle. He was helpless and she was the only person within miles who could assist him. If she didn’t do something to help him, who knows how long they might be stuck there in the middle of nowhere before help would reach them. And she sure did not want to make her way back to civilization by herself.

She looked at the container of pepper spray. It said to rinse the eyes out with water and get medical treatment promptly. She picked up his water bottle.

“Lie back,” she said.

"No," he said, pushing her away as she tried to help him. "Stay away from me. You did it to me again. Leave me alone."

"Collin," she began. "I have your water bottle. I have to rinse the spray out of your eyes."

She tilted his head back and pulled his arm away from his face. It alarmed her how red and swollen his eyes and face were, especially along the scars around his left eye.

His one hand reached out and locked around her wrist, as if he needed to brace himself.

She poured some water into one eye, then the other one, trying to wash out the chemicals. She took his second bottle of water and used most of that one also. She saved the remaining water to moisten her new bandanna and placed the cloth over his eyes.

"I have to go get my pack," she said, putting her hand on his shoulder. "Don't go anywhere."

Don't go anywhere? Collin shook his head. She was completely nuts. Where was he going to go? He couldn't see a thing.

"You have to let go of my arm," she said. "My pack is back on the trail."

He hadn't realized he had grasped her arm and he let it go.

The burning and throbbing in his eyes subsided only temporarily when she poured the water in them, but now the burning returned.

He pressed her moistened bandanna against his eyes and hoped she would get back quickly.

It seemed to take forever for her to return, but when she did, she emptied both of her water bottles, trying to remove the remaining pepper spray from his eyes.

"I can't believe you did this to me," Collin said to her. "I can't believe you did this."

"It was an accident."

"No," he said, pressing the bandanna against his eyes. "How can you *accidentally* spray pepper spray in somebody's face? It hurts so bad. I hate you."

"You're not making this easy for me," said the girl.

"Easy for you? You've made this nothing but hell for me. This was going to be the best thing and you totally destroyed it."

"Hey, what are you two lovebirds quarrelling about?" said a voice with a southern accent.

Brooke jumped, startled to see two hikers coming towards them from out of the fog.

"We are not lovers," said Brooke, insulted.

"Hell, no," said Collin.

"Are you all right there?" said another southern voice as he approached Collin.

"No," said Collin. "She maced me and I can't see. My eyes are burning something fierce."

"What did you do that for?" the first hiker asked Brooke.

"Because she's a spoiled pampered princess," said Collin, surprising himself at how fast he said it.

"Then you must be the Juvenile Delinquent," said the second hiker, patting him on his shoulder. "You two make a great pair. You'll probably kill each other before you reach Duncannon."

Collin groaned and the southern boys helped him sit up.

"We got a cell phone," said the first one. "I wouldn't leave home without it. By the way, my name's One and this is Two. I'm One because I always get into the shelters first, and Two's always second getting in."

One dialed 911 and told the operator they were on the Appalachian Trail more than a mile north of the Arendstville-Shippensburg Road.

"Help is on the way," said One, putting his cell phone away.

"Thank God," said Collin. "When we get back, I'm going straight to that judge and telling him that there's laws against cruel and unusual punishment. I've had it with you, Princess. I don't want to be near you for one more inch let alone another hundred miles."

"Look," said Brooke feeling the intensity of his anger. "It wasn't my…"

"Don't say it," said Collin angrily stopping her. "Don't say it wasn't your fault. It was totally one hundred percent your fault."

He thought back at all that had happened from the moment she came speeding around the curve and slammed into him. Lying on the asphalt road, unable to breathe or move. The intense pain and fear he felt. Then recovering, locked-up in juvenile jail and being sentenced to hike with the girl who had done this to him. And now his eyes and face were burning in pain and he couldn't see.

"She hits me with her car and nearly kills me… and now she did this…" Collin told the two boys, his voice cracking.

"You did that to him?" One asked her. "You hit him with your car?"

"Well," she began. "It was just…"

"Were you drunk or something?" Two asked her.

"No," she said. "Maybe I was going a little fast..."

"She was speeding," said Collin.

"Let me see your eyes," said One trying to pry the bandanna away from his face.

"That's pretty nasty," he said, seeing the red swelling around Collin's eyes.

"Wow," said Two, glancing over to Brooke. "You're one cold person."

Hurt and startled by the hikers' comments, Brooke shook her head. Why did she let their words bother her like this? She never cared before what people said about her. Never. Why did it bother her now? Brooke stared at the thru-hikers.

"Look," she began. "My folks have a lot of money. They'll pay for his hospital expenses and they'll reimburse you for your help."

"What's money got to do with it?" One asked. "Do you think money is going to solve all your problems?"

"There's nothing wrong with money," said Brooke.

"Of course there's nothing wrong with money," One agreed.

"You're just jealous of me," she said.

"Jealous of you?" One asked. "No. No, Princess. You have nothing that I would be jealous of."

Collin felt a tap on his shoulder.

"Think maybe you could walk a little?" One asked him. "We can go meet them at the gate we passed."

Collin nodded and the two hikers helped him to his feet.

"Where's my pack?" he asked.

"Right here," said Two, helping him put it over his shoulders.

"I wanted to hike the A.T. since spring," Collin told them. "I just didn't expect it would be like this."

"You never know what the next mile will bring," said Two. "Or the next hill or the next town. It's usually a pretty darn good thing. I don't think I ever ran into someone who's had as much trouble as you have had."

"Did you get to see McAfee Knob?" Collin asked them.

"Yeah," said One. "We were there. The view was awesome."

"The view from Dragon's Tooth was pretty awesome, too," said Two. "Some days you can see forever, some days there is no view at all, like today."

"You're going to be okay, J.D.," One said, trying to comfort Collin.

"J.D.?" Collin asked.

"Yeah, J.D., you know, short for Juvenile Delinquent."

"But I'm not a Juvenile Delinquent," said Collin.

"How did you get your name?" asked One.

"The Spoiled Little Princess gave it to me."

"So, are you or aren't you a delinquent?" One asked.

"I skipped school and ran away to hike the A.T."

The hikers looked at each other.

"And that's why you're in all this trouble?" they asked him.

He nodded.

"And what about your father?" Brooke said, then regretted saying it.

"And what about yours?" Collin asked. "How could he possibly have a daughter as mean and as heartless as you?"

A rescue jeep met them and a paramedic washed Collin's eyes with a sterile solution.

"You'll be fine once the swelling goes down," said the paramedic. "There's an ambulance waiting on the road. We'll get you to the hospital and have a doctor check you out."

He helped Collin into the back seat of the jeep and jumped in beside him.

"Take care, J.D." One called out to Collin. "Bet you never thought you'd be yellow-blazing in an ambulance. We'll be heading for the Tagg Run Shelter tonight, so we won't be seeing you. But good luck. Hope you make it back to the trail okay."

"Thanks," said Collin. "Thanks for everything."

"Hey," said Two. "The trail will always be here. It's not going anywhere. I know you wanted to do the whole thing, but if it doesn't work right now, it'll be here when you can do it."

"Ready," said the rescue jeep driver.

"Let's go," said the paramedic.

"Hey, wait for me," said Brooke as she jumped into the empty front seat.

Three hours after Collin was admitted to the emergency room, he was released with a small container of eye drops. His eyes were still red, but the swelling had started to go down.

He glared at Brooke as he reached for his pack that was by her side.

"I filled your water bottles," she said.

"Good-bye," he said, taking them from her. "I hope I never see you again."

"Wait," she said. "What are you doing? Where are you going?"

"I'm going as far away from you as I can get. Australia, New Zealand, maybe."

"But what about our sentence?"

"Sentence? C'mon, Brooke, you know this was just for show. For your Dad's political future."

"What do you mean?"

"Don't be stupid," he said. "This was all just a set up to see if they could do something about the future president's spoiled child. Well, they can play their games with somebody else. I'm out of here."

"You're wrong," Brooke screamed at him. "You were right in the same courtroom I was when the judge told us we had to do this. My father told me he couldn't do anything about it. And my father wouldn't lie to me!"

"Whatever, Brooke. Just leave me alone."

Collin took off down the street with his thumb out, looking for a ride to get him as fast and as far away from the Princess as he could get.

But no one pulled over to give him a ride. After half an hour of walking, a police car drove up. The cop made him get in the car and took him to the local police station.

Without even reading him his rights, the cop placed him in a jail cell in the back of the building and locked the door. Collin was surprised but glad to see Brooke was sitting in a cell across from him. Her head was down and Collin could tell she had been crying.

"Welcome to my world, Princess," he said. "How do you like your visit to the dungeon?"

She glared up at him briefly but then looked away.

"It's not fun when you're not free," he said.

He sat down on his bunk watching her. She sat with her head down. They did not say another word to each other.

After twenty minutes a sergeant came in.

"You two have two choices. One, you can go back and finish what the judge ordered the two of you to do. Or, two, you can both be sent to the State Correctional Institute for Juvenile Delinquents."

"It's safer in here, than out there with her," said Collin. "I'll pick the jail time."

"No," Brooke cried out. "I can't be locked up like an animal."

"Make up your minds," said the sergeant. "You must both agree on what you're going to do."

"J.D.," Brooke cried to him. "I can't be locked up. It's even worse than that awful nature stuff, but I'd rather be out there than be locked up."

"I'm not J.D.," he said to her. "I'm not a juvenile delinquent."

Collin glanced up at the cop. The cop seemed to think otherwise.

"I bet you don't even know what my real name is," Collin said to Brooke.

"It's... it's..." she paused. "Cory."

"It's Collin," he said, correcting her.

"Please, Collin," she said. "I don't want to be in here. Let's just go and get this over with."

"I want you to apologize, first."

"For what?" she asked.

"For everything."

"No, I can't apologize. I can't..."

"Apologizing is the least thing you could do," said the sergeant listening to them.

"But I never apologized to anyone about anything ever before in my whole entire life."

"Then there's a first time for everything," the sergeant said.

She paced her cell then stood directly across from Collin.

"Look," she began. "Setrees don't regret anything. Don't you understand?"

"No," said Collin. "Not in a million years."

"All right," she said. "I'm…. I'm sorry." She took a deep breath. "There I said it. Now let me out of here."

"Miss Setree," the sergeant began, "You can do a lot better than that. That sounded so insincere."

Brooke threw her hands up in the air and tried to compose herself. She paced back and forth in her cell and bit her lower lip. A tear fell down her face and she quickly brushed it away. She stopped pacing and began to speak, unable to look at Collin.

"Collin," she began. "I'm…" She stopped and brushed back another tear.

The sergeant stared at Brooke. Was she crying because she regretted what she had done to Collin or because she was locked in a jail cell and being forced to apologize?

"I'm sorry I hit you with the car," the girl continued. "I'm sorry you got hurt. I'm sorry I sprayed you with the pepper spray. I was scared when I couldn't see you in the fog. I heard that rustling noise and I thought there was a killer out there. I'm sorry."

"Okay," said Collin. "Do me a favor and keep your distance. Like say fifty feet."

"All right," she said.

"Okay," said the sergeant releasing them. "I'll have one of my men drop you off at the trailhead. I don't want any more trouble from either of you. Do you understand? A lot of people are keeping an eye on you both."

They were dropped off right where they were picked up earlier that day, but before they got started Collin turned to Brooke.

"Where's that little canister of pepper spray you carry?"

"The police took it."

"Good," he said to her. "Now, we can continue."

Chapter 13

They had only gone a total of six miles that day when they stopped at the Toms Run Shelter for the night.

One and Two had taken up a whole page in the register writing about how Juvenile Delinquent got pepper sprayed by the Spoiled Little Princess.

"This is awful," said Brooke, about to tear the page out.

"Hey," said a hiker who came walking up to the shelter. "You can't do that."

"But it's awful. It's not true."

The hiker took off his pack and took the notebook from her and read what One and Two wrote about Brooke. Then he saw Collin's face.

"You maced him? Seriously?" he said to Brooke. "How could you do a thing like that? The others aren't going to believe this."

"What others?" Brooke asked him.

"My friends," he said. "We've been hiking together since Springer. We are the Springer 8."

Brooke looked up to see a pack of seven more hikers, all in their twenties, come strolling up to the Toms Run Shelter.

"It's a whole mob," she said to Collin.

The first hiker didn't waste any time in passing the register around to his friends. They all read how the Spoiled Little Princess pepper sprayed the Juvenile Delinquent.

"This isn't true. It can't be," said one of the hikers until he saw Collin, his face and eyes still red from her attack. "I can't believe she did that to you."

They all stared at Brooke.

"I was scared," said Brooke trying to defend herself. "It was foggy. I heard this rustling."

"And what was it?" a hiker asked her.

Brooke was slow to answer. She looked over at Collin and back at the hikers.

"It was a chipmunk," she said quietly.

"A chipmunk?" they asked her.

She nodded and everyone but Brooke broke out laughing.

"Wow, you are one wild child," said one of the hikers. "I'm glad I'm not hiking with you." He looked over at Collin. "You can hook up with us any time. But that girl has got to go."

Collin looked over at Brooke. She moved away from the rest of the hikers to be by herself.

After everyone had finished eating, Collin and the eight thru-hikers sat around in a big circle talking about the half-gallon challenge.

"What are you talking about?" Brooke asked them from outside their circle.

They all looked in her direction. At first no one wanted to talk to her, but finally one hiker spoke up.

"The half-gallon challenge is a way of celebrating the midway point between Georgia and Maine. Thru-hikers will eat or at least attempt to eat a half-gallon of ice cream at the store in Pine Grove Furnace State Park."

"What's the midway point of Pennsylvania?" she asked them moving closer.

"Probably around Rausch Gap," one of the hikers told her. "But the midway point of the whole trail is just a mile or two past the ice cream."

"What's yellow blazing?" she asked them next.

"That's what slackers do when they skip a piece of trail by hitching a ride. You're following the yellow blaze down the middle of the road instead of the white blazes on the trail."

"Who's yellow blazing?" another hiker asked her.

"This guy named One told us we were yellow-blazing in an ambulance," Brooke said. "But we didn't skip any of the trail."

"We hiked with One and Two down south," said another hiker, "but we haven't seen them since the Shenandoahs. We heard they slack-packed Maryland, to do the Maryland Challenge."

"Wonder if they took a zero day after doing a forty mile day?" said another hiker.

Brooke moved away from the circle. There were too many hikers talking too much hiker talk. She went to the far corner of the shelter, got into her sleeping bag and closed her eyes.

The next morning they entered Pine Grove Furnace State Park and stopped at the little grocery store. It was full of hikers all eating ice cream at ten o'clock in the morning.

"I was dreaming about this all last night," said one of the hikers.

"That's disgusting," Brooke said to the hikers. "Stuffing your face with all that ice cream."

"You don't get it, Princess," said Collin. "This is a famous, well-known Appalachian Trail tradition. It's part of the hiking lore, like a rite of passage."

"Here," said a hiker placing a half gallon of vanilla ice cream into Collin's hands. "We took up a collection."

"Wow, thanks," Collin said and began eating it.

He tried but couldn't keep up with the thru-hikers. They were finished by the time he had eaten only half of his ice cream.

"You gotta finish it," the hikers told him. "We're not leaving until you do."

"Okay, okay," said Collin working his way to the bottom of the container.

When he finished the last spoonful they headed out together.

What a friendly group, Collin thought to himself. Not one of the eight knew any of the others before they had started hiking, but now they kept together. Sometimes they got split apart on the trail during the day, but then they always met up at the same shelter each night. One guy was from Canada, one was from England, and the others had come from six different states around the country. Collin knew those eight hikers would be friends for life. This touched Collin. This strong bond that these friends had was what Collin himself wished he had. But this time out, there would be no chance for Collin to form this type of friendship. He was stuck hiking with the nasty Princess and her impossibly slow pace.

He would be sorry to see the Springer 8 leave, but they would soon be off and out of sight. Their pace was ten times faster than anything Collin could do hiking with Brooke.

Collin and the group stopped at the old Pine Grove Furnace, a huge stone furnace from the 1700s for making iron. The furnace dwarfed the hikers as they stood near it to have their picture taken.

Brooke watched them from a distance. They were laughing and acting like little kids.

She waited at a picnic table as they left the trail to go up a grassy knoll to visit the Appalachian Trail Museum located in what had been the big old Pine Grove Furnace grist mill.

They were inside for half an hour.

"You missed it," one of the hikers told her when they came back out.

"What did I miss?"

"An original shelter built by Earl Shaffer."

"Who's he?"

"You don't know who Earl Shaffer was?"

"No," she said.

"He was the first person who ever hiked the trail in one continuous trek. He was the very first thru-hiker. He did it back in 1948. It helped him to deal with the post-traumatic stress that he suffered from what he had experienced in World War II."

"That's nice," she said, feigning interest.

He shrugged and rejoined his friends as they followed the trail over to Fuller Lake where they all jumped in for a quick swim before continuing their walk.

The trail through the park couldn't have been easier, but once again the footpath began going uphill and Collin saw the hikers stop up ahead at a large wooden sign on their left. They had reached the Appalachian Trail midpoint marker. The sign read: *Appalachian Trail, Maine to Georgia. Springer Mountain 1090.5 S. Mt. Katahdin 1090.5 N.*

All of the thru-hikers stopped to have their picture taken at it.

While Collin and Brooke watched them, one of the thru-hikers asked if Collin could take their group picture.

"Hey," one of the hikers joked loudly, "make sure you get that camera back from him. Word on the trail is that he's a Juvenile Delinquent."

Brooke looked over at Collin wondering what he thought of their taunts, but Collin was smiling, too. They were purely joking around with him. He looked happy, happier than she had ever seen him.

"Hey, I want to get a picture with the Juvenile Delinquent," some of the others called out.

"And the Spoiled Little Princess," the others said.

They pushed Collin and Brooke into the center of the photo then asked another hiker going past to stop and take their pictures.

After several minutes of picture taking they all continued again up the trail. For a while some of the thru-hikers walked with Collin and Brooke, but they were used to going at a much faster pace and it wasn't long before they were saying good-bye. One by one they threw their arms around Collin. Then as they all passed Brooke they each bowed down as if before royalty.

As the first one bowed Brooke stood there with her arms crossed and an angry look on her face.

When the fourth hiker bowed down, the hiker from England stopped him and hit him with his hiking pole.

"Ahh, do that again, peasant, I done told you how to do it proppa," he said in an exaggerated cockney accent.

The frown in Brooke's face cracked for an instant as the errant hiker bowed a second time. When the last of the eight thru-hikers performed their bows, they all took off and were gone.

Their voices faded into the distance and the quietness that descended was incredible. The trail was suddenly a very empty place.

"We'll never see them again," Collin said, mostly to himself, but Brooke heard him. "Out here people come into your lives for a brief intense human moment and then they are gone forever."

Brooke noticed a silence in Collin after the hikers took off. He was always a good thirty paces ahead of her but now he was hanging back almost by her side.

They came to a wood sign on a tree. It said *Pole Steeple*.

"Are you checking this out?" Brooke said to Collin.

"No. It's a half mile out and another back. We'll just keep going."

They walked on in silence for a time and then Collin spoke up.

"I guess you're used to being in front of the cameras, like back there at that sign."

"Yeah, it's no big deal." she said. "There's always paparazzi around."

"Like when we started back at Pen Mar?"

"Yeah, I can't wait to see how I look in those photos. I guess you've seen me on magazine covers."

"No," he said. "Are you a model or something?"

"Are you joking? Don't you know who I am?"

"You are the daughter of a senator."

"Is that all you know about me?"

"Yeah. And you had lots of luggage back at Pen Mar, so that means you must have lots of clothes. Where do you get all your money from?"

“My mom owns several corporations and she inherited a huge amount. My dad works too, but it’s my mom that has the real money.”

“Your dad works, too?” he said, repeating her words. “He’s a senator! You make it sound like he’s just a regular blue collar guy.”

“Well, it obviously doesn’t matter how much money either of them make, because I’m still out here.”

They walked on, hiking a total of eleven miles that day until they stopped for the night at the Tagg Run Shelter.

Brooke watched as Collin glanced around, looking for any sign that the large group had already come in and set up camp. But there was no one there.

“I guess they blew by here,” he said aloud. “They’re probably doing another eight miles to get to the Alex Kennedy Shelter.”

“Yeah, I guess,” she said, not caring whether or not the group was there.

Brooke picked up the trail register and began to write.

How many more nights must I spend in these awful little shelters? I want a real bed and four walls around me. Brooke.

She put the notebook down and picked up the map of the section they would be doing tomorrow.

“There’s six mountains we have to climb?” she gasped horrified.

“Let me see that,” Collin said, taking the map from her. “These are tiny little hills. These aren’t massive climbs. Don’t make a big thing out of it. And check this out, after we come off Center Point Knob, there isn’t another uphill for at least fifteen miles.”

"For real?" she said, taking the map back and studying it.

Collin watched as a smile crossed her face.

"Wow," she said. "Look how flat. Good!" She was silently studying it and then spoke up. "But there's no shelters in this stretch. Nothing from Alex Kennedy to the Darlington Shelter."

"There's camping just outside Boiling Springs. We'll stay there and then we'll take those next fifteen or so miles in a flash."

"Fifteen miles? That's a really long piece."

"But it's flat," said Collin.

He picked up the register and moved away to write his entry.

After he cooked his dinner, Collin lay down in his sleeping bag and pulled out his trail guidebook to read by the light of his headlight. He heard some hikers come in to camp and he looked up. It was three girls.

"Hey, how's it going?" they said to Brooke.

"It would be a lot better if I was spending my summer someplace else. Like on the beach."

"Don't tell me you're the Spoiled Little Princess?" said the first girl who carried a doll with long blond hair on the side of her pack.

"I guess I am," said Brooke.

"So where's the Juvenile Delinquent?"

"He's in the shelter already. He never turns in this early, but he did tonight."

"We'll just give him a quick hi, then," said the oldest girl.

All three girls left her and went over to say hello to Collin. He greeted them back, but they didn't linger. They gave him his space and got busy making their dinner.

After they ate, they sat around with Brooke.

"So what's with the doll?" Brooke asked them.

"Her name is Goldilocks," said the youngest girl. "And we're the Three Bears."

"You look like you could be sisters. Are you?" Brooke asked.

"Yeah, and our real last name is Baer," said the youngest sister. "We didn't start out with the doll, but everyone kept saying, oh look it's the three Baers. So we became the Three Bears. Then someone asked, where's Goldilocks? We figured we had to get a Goldilocks to hike with us so we bought the doll at a store down in Damascus."

"You went shopping," said Brooke. "Except for my smartphone, my bed, and my bathroom, I miss shopping most of all. How far away is Damascus?"

"Oh, that's about 600 miles back, near the very southwest corner of Virginia."

"Why would you choose to be out here doing this?" Brooke asked. "I find it disgusting not having a hot bath every day."

"We just like the outdoors," said the youngest one.

"How old are you?" Brooke asked her.

"I'm 17. My name's Jessica. When I heard my sisters talking about hiking the Appalachian Trail I told them I was going to come along whether they wanted me to or not."

"We kept trying to lose her, but she kept finding us," said the oldest one smiling. "I'm Ashley. I'm 22."

"I'm Emily. I'm 19."

"I don't get this at all," said Brooke. "I don't understand why you're doing this and enjoying it."

"I like the challenge," said Ashley. "And it's a big goal to get to Katahdin in Maine and we're halfway there. It's going to be something we'll remember all our lives and to do it together is huge."

"My friends think I'm crazy," said Jessica, "They can't believe I'm out here doing this. They think it's scary to be out here, but it's been great. It's been an adventure they will never understand and will never experience."

"I don't want to wake up one day and be seventy years old and think I never did anything big in my life," said Emily. "I don't want to have any regrets for not trying things and really living."

"When you're out here you feel so alive and one with nature," said Ashley.

"But don't you ever get tired?" said Brooke. "Don't you ever want to get in a car or go shopping?"

"Sure," said Jessica. "But this isn't a forced march. We're doing it because it is fun. We wouldn't be out here if it wasn't fun. I love my sisters and after we finish at Katahdin, it will be a long time until we will see each other again. Ashley heads back to school in California and Emily will be going to college in Florida and I have to go back home to Minnesota to finish high school."

"Talk about an intense bonding experience," said Ashley. "This is it."

"Don't you have any brothers or sisters?" Emily asked her.

"No," said Brooke.

"Hasn't anything been fun for you on this hike?" Jessica asked her.

"Having my picture taken at the halfway mark was fun. It reminded me of my real life."

"I read your register entries," said Jessica reaching for the shelter notebook. "They're interesting. But we really like what the Juvenile Delinquent writes."

"Did he write one in there?" Emily asked.

"Yeah," said Jessica and she began to read it aloud. "*Having someone to laugh with is the best thing there is out here and back in the real world where you need it even more. The lighthearted friendship and real camaraderie between people is a treasure worth more than a million dollars. We're all on the same trail of life; sometimes it is difficult and steep and rocky, but having someone to laugh with ... it just doesn't get any better than that. I got to hike with some really awesome guys today. They bought me a half-gallon of ice cream and I ate all of it. Thanks for making this the best day out on the trail, guys. Juvenile Delinquent.*"

"That's nice," said Emily. "I hope he writes a whole book after he finishes the trail."

"He's really into all of this," said Brooke. "I'm not." She yawned. "I'm turning in now, too."

"Good night," they said to her.

Jessica wrote an entry for Goldilocks and the Three Bears then returned the notebook to the register box.

Brooke climbed into her sleeping bag. For a while she watched Collin as he read his book on the opposite end of the shelter. He was just so different than anyone she had ever met. At one point he looked over in her direction and for a moment they stared at each other.

"Good night," he said to her and switched off his light.

The next morning the Three Bears had already left the shelter by the time Brooke and Collin got on the trail. They began to climb and found themselves on a section known as Rocky Ridge. They were soon scrambling through the most massive boulders they had yet encountered. Up till now they watched for the blazes on the trees, but as they passed through the maze of rock formations, they watched for the white blazes on the edges of the giant boulders.

"I'd like to see you try this in your heels," said Collin.

"The next time I wear heels is at my welcome home party that my friends will be throwing for me the first night I am out of here."

They hiked on and passed by a wooden sign posted high on a tree.

"Look, it's the Western Terminus of the Mason-Dixon Trail," said Collin, pointing to the sign.

"I'm so glad you told me that," said Brooke. "I don't know how I could have lived without that important piece of information."

"Princess, I've had it with your sarcastic comments."

"Well, then stop making your stupid comments."

They reached a blue-blazed trail. A little wooden sign high on a tree told them they had come 8.2 miles from the Tagg Run Shelter and the Alec Kennedy Shelter was two-tenths of a mile off the trail.

As they walked down the blue-blazed trail, Brooke spoke up.

"Why do they have to put these shelters so far off the trail?" she asked.

"Two-tenths of a mile is not that far."

"Yes it is. I'll be glad when we get there."

They reached the shelter and signed in.

Brooke was ready to stop there for the night and started to open her sleeping bag.

"What are you doing?" he said. "We're not staying here. We only went eight miles today. I told you we were going to that campsite outside Boiling Springs. It's only about three more miles."

"Oh, all right," she said, rolling her sleeping bag back up and putting it away.

They began walking again and reached Center Point Knob.

"Look," said Collin pointing to a cairn behind a tree.

"What is it?" Brooke asked him.

"People wrote messages on these rocks."

There was a small pile of rocks where people had written messages in black marker. Some rocks had people's names, some poems, some just messages.

Hike on, it said on one of the rocks.

Another one said, *Just one small rock in the trail of life.*

Maine, here I come, read a third.

Collin read a few more before continuing on.

They hiked down off Center Point Knob and entered the long flat Cumberland Valley of Pennsylvania. They were no longer in the mountains hiking in the green tunnel of trees.

Walking through the open fields of corn seemed strange to Collin.

"This doesn't even feel like we are on the Appalachian Trail," he said. "Where are the rocks? Where are the trees?"

Collin turned around to see where they had been.

"Look back," he said. "That's the mountain we were just on."

Brooke glanced back, but as usual, she could care less.

"I'm glad there are no mountains up ahead," said Brooke looking in front of them.

"None for another fifteen miles."

They followed the well-worn path through the fields. Since there were no trees, the white blazes that marked the way of the Appalachian Trail were painted on fence posts.

On the south side of town was the campsite where they stopped for the night.

"I'm not camping here," said Brooke. "I'm going to stay in town tonight. I'm going to find a hotel room or a bed and breakfast."

"I'll see you tomorrow, then," said Collin.

But just over an hour later, she was back.

"What are you doing here?" he asked her.

"They wouldn't accept my charge card. It was declined. I am so angry. They wouldn't even let me use their phone to call the bank."

She unrolled her sleeping bag and sat down on it.

"Life is just so brutal," Collin said, mocking her.

She glared at him then turned her back to him.

"Maybe you can handle being poor, but I can't," she said.

He heard her crying softly and he walked over to her.

"You're not poor. You have everything."

She heard what he said and turned and looked up at him.

"Did you hear me?" he asked her. "You have so much. You're so lucky, more lucky than you will ever know. Quit feeling sorry for yourself."

He walked away from her, totally disgusted with her and her poor little rich girl attitude.

Chapter 14

The next morning they signed in at the register box outside the mid-Atlantic office of the Appalachian Trail Conservancy in Boiling Springs, filled their water bottles and continued walking through the flat farmland of the great valley.

They went up and down stiles as they crossed the fences that divided farmers' fields. Sometimes they hiked through fields of cows. Sometimes the pastures were empty. They crossed the bridge over the Pennsylvania Turnpike and walked through an enclosed footbridge and then yet another bridge over busy Interstate 81.

The white blazes were always there, on the side of a fence, on the edge of a bridge, but there was always another one in sight further up the trail.

Late in the day they crossed under the Route 944 pedestrian tunnel and left the long flat section of the Cumberland Valley farmland behind them as once again they began climbing.

They came to a sign for the Tuscarora Trail.

"Wonder what that trail's like?" Collin said, looking over at Brooke.

"I don't even want to know. This is the only trail I must be on and I could care less about any other ones."

They took a right at a blue blaze and headed to the Darlington Shelter for the night.

The next day as they came down off the mountain, they entered fields surrounded by trees.

"Do you know what this means?" Brooke whined to Collin. "It means we'll have to go back uphill again."

"Yeah," said Collin, pointing ahead of them as they came into another open field. "There it is, but it doesn't look that bad."

"It looks bad enough," she said.

They crossed Route 850 and the trail seemed to descend even further as they crossed the last field. Just after they entered the trees they began a slow uphill climb. Up on the ridge, five miles from the road, they reached the next shelter.

"There used to be another shelter here," Collin said to Brooke. "You can still see the outline of its base. It was the Thelma Marks Shelter, but this new one is called the Cove Mountain Shelter."

Brooke expressed her disinterest to Collin's comments with a loud yawn.

Collin shook his head and turned his attention to the register and picked up a pen.

We are almost to Duncannon, he wrote. *Almost to the Susquehanna River. We have crossed little creeks but no big rivers. Can't wait to see it. Juvenile Delinquent.*

He handed the notebook to Brooke and all she did was sign her name.

The next two miles seemed long to Collin, but only because he was anxious to reach the overlook called Hawk Rock. In forty minutes they were there.

"Wow," said Collin. "Check this out. You can see where the Juniata joins the Susquehanna River."

"How do you know what river that is?"

"I read about it in the guidebook," he said. "And it's on the map."

From their mountaintop view they could see far into the valley below them and see the confluence of the two rivers.

"You knew that, though, didn't you?" he said to her.

"No. How would I?"

"We're just north of Harrisburg. Isn't that where you live?"

"Yeah, but I don't know things like rivers and mountains."

"Well, here's a 411 about this mountain we're on. This next mile coming up that takes us down off the mountain is going to be pretty steep, so be careful."

They began their descent off the mountain. It was steep, even with the switchbacks.

At the base of the mountain they entered the town of Duncannon. They stopped long enough to get a soda and some snacks in a convenience store with Collin's limited supply of money and moved on.

"Hey, Princess! Juvenile Delinquent!" someone called to them. It was Tennessee Tara. "Me and some of my friends rented a room at the Hiker Bistro and Bar. There's a whole bunch of hikers there who have been taking zero days for this big party tonight. You can stay with us if you want."

Collin and Brooke looked at each other.

"It's a famous hiker hangout," Collin said to her. "It wouldn't be right to miss this opportunity."

Brooke shrugged.

"I don't care," she said. "As long as I can get a shower."

They followed Tennessee Tara to the two-story building in the cul-de-sac off the main street. Behind the back of the building where the hikers had gathered, a large bonfire had been built. Hikers were eating and drinking and someone was playing a guitar.

"There's free food inside," said Tennessee Tara. "Stash your packs up in 204 and load up on whatever you like. Some thru-hiker from last year is putting on this spread for all thru-hikers."

"Cool," said Collin. "But we're not thru-hikers."

"No, but you have the spirit of a thru-hiker."

"Thanks," he said.

Collin and Brooke made their way inside. Hikers and townies were drinking at the bar. In the back room, Collin saw some hikers playing pool.

They went up the stairs and found the room.

Opening the door they found ten backpacks already on the floor.

"What's a zero day?" Brooke asked him.

"When a thru-hiker doesn't do any hiking. They take a day off and therefore go zero miles that day."

"Wish we could take a few zero days now and then," said Brooke.

The room did not look like it could accommodate more than six hikers, let alone twelve.

"Do you want to stay here?" Collin asked Brooke.

"As long as I can get a shower."

"Are you going to go down to the bonfire?" he asked her.

"No, I'm tired," said Brooke. "And those aren't the kind of people I like to party with. Are you going?"

"Heck, yeah. There's free food. I'm going to eat and hang out a while. Maybe play some pool."

"Yeah, maybe I'll go for the food, too."

"I think I'll get a shower before I go down," said Collin. "It will probably be a long wait line later. You go first, if you want. I'll wait till you're done."

After they got cleaned up, they went downstairs together and found they were the youngest hikers in the place.

Collin grabbed a hamburger, two hot dogs and some barbecued chicken, and after he ate out at the bonfire, he went back inside to play a game of pool.

"You look great, Princess," Tennessee Tara said. "Check out your legs. What did I tell you? Did you ever think that walking could get you in such great shape?"

"That's probably the only good thing about being out here," said Brooke.

"What about your friend, the Juvenile Delinquent? Isn't he one of the good things about being out here?"

"He's not my friend."

"Why not?"

"We're different. Besides, we both hate each other."

"No, don't say that," said Tennessee Tara. "How can you hate each other while you're out on this journey together? The Juvenile Delinquent is a very cool kid to want to be out here doing this."

"We're just too different."

Collin shot some pool with some of the other hikers and stayed a while to eat some more of the free buffet, but as it got later and later and the beer drinkers out-numbered the soda drinkers, he went over to Brooke and told her he was going upstairs.

"Are you being my babysitter, now?" she asked him.

"No, I was just telling you I was heading upstairs."

She rolled her eyes, but then decided to follow him anyway.

He crawled over a number of other sleeping bags till he reached his and climbed into it.

She went to the window and looked out.

"There's going to be a lot of people sleeping in here tonight," she said to Collin, moving her sleeping bag over to the window. "There's no air-conditioning. It will probably get really warm in here. I'm staying near the window."

He sat up and looked over at her. She was right.

"Yeah," he said. "That side of the room is better."

He grabbed his sleeping bag and moved it over to her side of the room and closed his eyes. The noise from the rowdy group below made it hard to get much sleep.

For the first time since they started their hike, Brooke and Collin slept in an enclosed room for the night and not out in the open night air.

The next morning Collin and Brooke were the first hikers up and out. Everyone else was still sleeping but he knew that sometime that day all the hikers would probably catch up to them.

The trail followed the long streets of the small town of Duncannon right along the Susquehanna River. It was the most road walking they had to do. It didn't even feel like they were on the trail with nothing but cement pavements under their feet and houses on both sides of the street.

"Seems strange," Collin spoke up. "Walking in town. Like where is that narrow green trail?"

"It's good to be able to walk without always having to watch where you put your feet," said Brooke, as she watched the phone poles for the white blazes.

"Do you think that the people who live here and see the hikers go by... do you think that they have any idea that people from all over the world are right here walking down their streets?"

"First, I don't care what these people here think. Second, what's the big deal?"

"There might be people who have lived here in this town all their lives and never got to see any of the places where these hikers are from. It's like they have these world travelers passing by their little Pennsylvania town. I think if I lived here I would stop every one of them and ask them about their country or their state, what their hometown is like and if they miss it and what they like about the trail, and a thousand other questions."

"I think that you need to get a life," she said.

"That's why I am out here, Princess."

At the end of town, they made a right and reached the first bridge and crossed over the Juniata River. Then they came to the next bridge, the long Clarks Ferry Bridge that crossed the wide Susquehanna River.

They paused in the middle of the span to look downriver.

"Look," said Collin, pointing into the distance off to their right. "That's the mountain we came down."

"I don't care so much about what we came down. Look at what we have to go up."

Ahead of them, across the river was a huge mountain.

"That's nothing," said Collin. "We'll be up that in no time at all."

They crossed the railroad tracks and began the climb up Peter's Mountain. It was a long, slow ascent with steep switchbacks.

Collin turned and looked back every so often. Brooke was not exactly keeping up with him, but she was going a lot faster than when she first started back in Pen Mar Park.

When they reached the Clarks Ferry Shelter they stopped briefly to sign the register and then kept going. They crossed a pedestrian bridge over Route 225. Below them cars sped around the curve on the mountain road.

"There wasn't always a bridge here," Collin said, watching the cars. "You can tell this is pretty new. The guidebook says that before this bridge was built old trail maps warned hikers that this was a very dangerous road crossing."

A car screeched around the mountaintop curve below them and Brooke looked over at Collin. She saw his shoulders tighten as he subconsciously braced himself. He took a deep breath and moved off the bridge.

By the time they reached the Peter's Mountain Shelter, their stop for the night, they had walked over eleven miles that day. The shelter was a two-story wood structure with a ladder that led to the second level loft.

Brooke immediately stowed her pack up there and stretched out her sleeping bag before descending the ladder to prepare her dinner.

She emptied a pouch of fettuccini pasta with beef and onion seasoning into her pan of water, and while it cooked, she looked up to see a group of hikers including Tennessee Tara come in from Duncannon.

After Brooke ate her dinner, she climbed up into the loft. Some hikers built a fire and everyone, except Brooke, sat up late talking.

From her cozy corner in the loft, Brooke heard them discussing Earl Shaffer and the shelter that he had built that was now on display in the Appalachian Trail Museum. Some of the hikers had not stopped at the museum. Those who did were debating its original location on the trail and she heard Collin speak.

"That little shelter that Earl built was located just a few steps from this one. We should look for a flat area in the light tomorrow morning and see if we can find where it stood. On that video it showed how a few years back, a bunch of the area trail maintaining clubs got together to preserve it for the museum. Forty people hiked in here that day. They disassembled that shelter and carried every log, piece by piece, out to that parking area we passed three miles back."

"They said it was the last surviving shelter that Earl himself built," another hiker added.

"Did you know people didn't believe that he had hiked the whole trail in one journey?" said Tennessee Tara. "If it wasn't for his journal and his photos, they weren't going to believe him."

Everyone else thought this was all fascinating, but Brooke didn't. It was just boring. Yet, she thought it was interesting how the Juvenile Delinquent held his own with the rest of these seasoned hikers. He knew so much about the trail and he fit right in with them.

She fell asleep with the voices of Collin and the others talking late into the night around the campfire.

Brooke was up first the next morning. There were hikers everywhere sleeping. She reached for the trail register and opened it to read what Collin wrote.

The walk across the Susquehanna River was amazing. We have three more major rivers to cross, but that was the widest one. I am anxious to get to the Delaware River but I will miss all you thru-hikers. Thanks for letting this section-hiker hang out with you. It's been fun! I wished I would have brought a journal with me so I can write down all your names. I am fitting what I can into the blank pages of my trail guidebook. I want to remember you all forever! Juvenile Delinquent.

She reached for the pen and added her own entry.

I can't say this hasn't been interesting, in a strange sort of way. I still don't understand why you would give up the real world to be here, Brooke wrote. She signed it, *Spoiled Little Princess*.

"Hey," said Tennessee Tara. "You done with that?"

"Yeah," said Brooke. She passed the notebook over to the thru-hiker who took the register and smiled at Brooke's entry before adding her five word response.

This is the real world! Tennessee Tara.

Collin said good-bye to Tennessee Tara and the other hikers and watched them as they left the Peter's Mountain Shelter and disappeared up the trail.

"They go so fast," said Brooke. "I wish I could go faster, too, so we could reach the end quicker."

"I wish we could keep up with them, too. I like having the other hikers around. But do you know what I really like? I really like sitting around a campfire at night talking with them. I didn't want last night to end."

"What's the big deal about having a fire? We have four fireplaces in our house," she said smugly, "but except for Christmas, we never sit in front of them. We have a fireplace in the back patio, too, but we're never home that much to use it."

"Don't you have cookouts with your friends and family during the summer?"

"We spend most of the summer at our place down at the shore."

"I can't even imagine what that's like."

"Are you jealous?"

"No," he said. "You don't understand. I think it's kind of sad how you live."

"Sad? Why would you say that?"

"You have what sounds like a really nice place, but you're not even there to enjoy it."

"When we are there, we enjoy it. And we enjoy our place at the shore even more."

"I couldn't handle having a place that awesome and not be there."

"You're never going to have a home that big anyway," she said in her most haughty and conceited tone yet. "So you won't ever have to worry about anything like that."

She knew how arrogant she sounded and she didn't care. She waited for his response, but he didn't say anything to her.

He had dealt with some cruel taunts from others in his life, but she was exceptionally mean. Why did she have to act like that out here on the trail where they were equals? He turned away from her and walked up the trail.

A little over five miles from the shelter, the trail began a long descent. Collin and Brooke came down off Peter's Mountain, crossed Route 325 and began a long climb up the trail onto Stony Mountain. Collin kept going, his momentum carrying him upward. Brooke walked slowly.

"How far up does this go?" Collin heard her call from far behind him.

After a while he heard her yelling again about the never ending trail up the mountainside.

Collin liked this section of trail. He felt so exhilarated and energized he couldn't stop or contain himself. He was practically running up the trail and he kept going even after he reached the ridgeline. It wasn't until Collin came to a plaque in the middle of the trail that he stopped. The plaque said this was where the Horseshoe Trail ended its 121 miles after beginning in Valley Forge.

"Horseshoe Trail," he said aloud. "It just doesn't have the same appeal as the Appalachian Trail."

Without a watch he did not know what time it was, but it seemed like they had been on the trail for at least a couple hours. He took out his trail map. He knew he had been going at a good pace. From what he was seeing on the map, it looked like he had gone over nine miles. There was another good eight miles to go until they reached the Rausch Gap Shelter.

He turned and looked down the trail from where he had come. Brooke was nowhere in sight. He wondered if she would be able to hike another eight miles today.

He sat down to take a break. Pulling out his food bag he ate some peanut butter crackers and a candy bar. He drank some water and still did not see Brooke.

"Are you coming?" he yelled down the trail.

There was no answer so he stretched out on the ground and closed his eyes. Sometime later he heard rustling and awoke to see Brooke, slowly approaching him with a big stick in her arms, poised like she was about to attack him with it.

Rattlesnakes, like this one on the boulders at the Eagle's Nest overlook, can be found on the Appalachian Trail in Pennsylvania.

Chapter 15

Brooke swung the stick directly at him.

"No," he yelled, putting his hands up in front of him to deflect the blow.

"I got it," she yelled.

He brought his arms down from his face in time to see something go flying through the air and land ten feet off the trail.

"What are you doing?" he yelled, jumping up.

"It was a huge rattlesnake," she said. "I hurled it away from you so you wouldn't get bit."

"You mean that snake over there?" he asked pointing to a dazed black snake.

She nodded.

"It's just a black snake. It's not poisonous."

"Well, if it was a rattlesnake, I just saved your life."

"You scared me," he said.

"I wasn't going to hit you!" she said angrily. "How mean do you think I am? No, wait, don't answer that."

"Princess, you can't be disturbing the wildlife out here. You can't be attacking snakes, like that. This is their home. We are just visiting here."

"You are too sensitive, J.D."

"And you are not sensitive enough. You are probably the least sensitive person I have ever met."

Collin looked at the stick she held tightly in her hand.

"So, when are you going to drop your stick?"

"I'm going to hold on to it. I don't like this section at all. It seems so much more creepy and silent than all the other places we've been."

"It's called St. Anthony's Wilderness. It is kind of remote, in fact, it's the longest stretch we'll be on where no road crosses near it. A long time ago, there used to be tiny villages near here, but they are now just ghost towns."

"I knew it was a creepy place. I want to get out of here. How far to the next shelter?"

"Eight miles," he said to her. "The next ridge we'll be on is Sharp Mountain. We'll go past the ruins of Yellow Springs Village and a few miles past that is the shelter."

"Another eight miles?" she asked.

"But it's mostly ridge walking. It'll be a piece of cake. Did you see that plaque back there for the Horseshoe Trail? All you have to do is follow it for 121 miles and you'll be in Valley Forge. Were you ever there?"

"All you have to do is follow it for 121 miles," she said mimicking him. "Do you hear what you are saying? You act like it's just a short little stroll away." She rolled her eyes. "Yes, as a matter of fact I have been to the King of Prussia Mall which is right near Valley Forge, but no, I have not been to Valley Forge. What's in Valley Forge anyway?"

"You don't know about Valley Forge?"

"I'm just joking with you. Of course I know about Valley Forge. How stupid do you think I am? You can't be a senator's daughter without learning all about the country and its history."

"So your dad is running for president?"

"My dad *is* going to be the next president," she stated.

"You seem really certain about that."

"I am. We all are. It was his plan from the beginning when he was in college. This year he's been popular in the polls, probably higher than he's ever been and he'll be popular in the voting booths in November. I'm going to live in the White House. And as stupid as you may think this is, I plan to be married there."

"That poor guy," Collin said quietly.

"What did you say?"

"I said, who are you going to marry?"

"I haven't decided yet."

"It must be nice to be a princess and to always be in control and have everything perfect and everything always work out for you."

"You don't think I had any control about this stupid hiking crap, do you?"

"Someone did," said Collin.

Angrily she stopped Collin and touched his arm.

"Don't say that," she said. "You're wrong. It was that stupid judge's fault that I'm here."

"That *we* are here."

She let go of his arm and continued walking.

"And what do you plan to do with your life?" she asked him. "But it's not like I really care, though."

"My plan is to get to the Delaware Water Gap and be free to keep going the rest of the way."

"I'm not talking about this and now. I'm talking about the next ten years, the rest of your life..."

"I don't know," he said. "I never thought about it."

"Haven't you ever dreamed about the future?"

"No, it's always just been nightmares about the present."

They walked another three miles before they came upon a wood post standing next to the trail. Attached to it was a sign and a mailbox.

The sign said *Yellow Springs, Old Coal Mining Village Ruins Circa 1850s*. The mailbox contained a trail register.

Collin opened the mailbox and pulled out the trail register.

"How come there's no shelter here?" Brooke whined.

"Because there isn't," was Collin's simple reply.

"That's a dumb answer."

"For a dumb question."

"How much farther is it to the shelter?" she asked.

"It's another four or five miles yet."

"Is it closer to four miles or closer to five miles?"

"Princess, do you have a nail appointment or some other incredibly important thing you have to get to?"

"I'm tired and four miles sounds a lot better than five miles."

"We have exactly 4.6 miles to the shelter. How does that sound?"

"Really long," she sighed.

They trudged into the Rausch Gap Shelter that evening. They had hiked eighteen miles that day. Some of the hikers that they had spent the previous night with were already there. Others had gone on even farther.

The Rausch Gap Shelter was newly built, replacing an old rotting structure. A pipe carrying water from a spring ran conveniently right in front of the shelter.

They cooked their meals in silence, both tired after their long day.

As his rice simmered and her au gratin potatoes cooked, Collin sat reading the register, when suddenly he looked up and around at the surrounding forest.

"What is it?" she asked.

"Just some of the entries. It says that a mama bear and her two cubs were being spotted here the last couple days."

"Bears?" Brooke asked. "I can't move another inch or else I'd be out of here."

"It will be all right," said Collin. "We'll just keep an eye out for them and hang our food up in a bear bag."

"A bear bag?"

"Yeah, like some of the others did already," he said, pointing to a couple bags that were suspended high from a nearby tree with a rope. "The bears can't reach it."

"But what about us? What if they come into the shelter?"

"Bears don't like to be around people," one of the other hikers told her. "Unless you have food in your sleeping bag they rarely ever come near people."

Collin was anxious to ask the other hikers if they had seen bears previously on the trail, but he thought Brooke was nervous enough already without hearing any more talk about them.

"Do you know what I hate about the nights out here?" she said later as she climbed into her sleeping bag. "It's so dark. There are no lights anywhere. No street lights. No lights from other houses. No car lights. No lights from inside a refrigerator."

"No refrigerators," one of the other hikers called out.

Even with thoughts of bears on her mind, Brooke slept soundly after their long exhausting day on the trail.

The next morning they left Sharp Mountain. They climbed up Second Mountain and then down the other side. Brooke kept her snake stick in her hand the entire way.

"I'm glad we didn't see any bears," she said. "But here we go with another downhill. That means another uphill is coming."

Between the mountains they crossed a large open field on a worn narrow single-file footpath. They were in Swatara Gap.

"Hey, check this out," said Collin, peering down at the long grass. "Look at the ends of the grass… those are ticks hanging off of them."

"That's disgusting," said Brooke. "Get out of my way." She pushed Collin aside and ran so fast across the field, Collin couldn't believe how fast she could go.

When he reached her a few minutes later, she stood waiting for him in the middle of the road.

"Are there any on me?" she asked hysterically. "I feel them all over me."

He looked at her and saw two black dots. Quickly he brushed off the ticks that were climbing up the back of her legs.

"Are you sure you got them all?" she asked.

"Yeah. I don't see any more."

"You don't know how much I hate being here."

"Yes, Princess, I do."

They walked over a long narrow bog bridge, crossed a road and followed the trail through a section of rhododendron. They came to an old iron bridge and crossed over Swatara Creek.

Reaching the support pylons of a bridge high above them, they looked up. It was Interstate 81.

A few days ago and some fifty miles back they had crossed over this interstate, but here they were now crossing underneath it.

The trail was heading up the mountain. Before long, they were level with the highway. With each step they took, they were soon above it and they kept climbing.

At the top of the mountain they looked through an opening in the trees and far below them they could see the highway as it stretched south away from the mountain. They could hear the traffic, especially the trucks, from a long distance.

"We're on the Blue Mountain, now," he told her.

"And why should I care about that?"

"We'll be on this mountain until near Delaware Water Gap, where the ridge is then called the Kittatinny Mountain which is an Indian word meaning 'endless mountain.'"

"Endless is a good name for all this."

"Yeah, yeah," he said quietly. "Complain, complain."

"What did you say?"

"All you do is whine. Why can't you see any of the good?"

"What good?"

"Look up at the blue sky. The weather is totally comfortable. It's not oppressively hot. The water sources have been good. We're lucky. It could be raining the whole time we are out here."

"You have a strange way of determining what's lucky and good. There is nothing good about this."

For several seconds he stared at her; she was so infuriating.

"Do you know what?" he began. "I can't take this any more. I don't want to be near you today. The William Penn Shelter will be off a side trail to your right in about 5 miles. I'm going ahead. Maybe I'll see you there. Maybe not. But I don't care. Just stay away from me."

He took off and she watched him disappear up the trail. She continued on alone on the ridge. The noise from the interstate became fainter and fainter until she no longer heard it.

She didn't like the silence. She didn't like being alone.

Somewhere overhead she heard a bird chirping. Later she saw two chipmunks cross the trail. She didn't expect to see a fawn, but there it was just off the trail to her left.

"You're cute," she said to it. She stood watching it for several minutes.

It stared at her, unmoving. It didn't seem to mind that she was there. Unconcerned by her presence it moved slowly through the brush.

"That was pretty cool," Brooke said.

She walked on another two miles and was surprised to see Collin. He was just standing there in the middle of the trail watching her. It looked like something was on his mind, but she couldn't really tell. He was wearing a game face, she thought. He had this serious, intense, determined look mixed with something else, maybe anger.

"What's up?" she asked cautiously.

"Nothing."

"How come you're not at the shelter?"

He shrugged but didn't answer.

Something was definitely going on with him but she didn't know what it was.

He let her go past him.

It was weird how he was walking behind her, she thought to herself. Maybe he was so angry with her that he was going to try something, like beat her up and leave her there so deep in the woods no one would ever find her. She knew from his family history that he was probably capable of anything. Feeling vulnerable, she hoped there would be some other hikers at the shelter.

When they finally reached the wooden hut, she was happy to see it, but no other hikers were there, not on the lower level, not up in the loft. Yesterday they did some major miles. Today they walked another thirteen. She felt exhausted and could not handle even the thought of walking one more step.

Warily she watched Collin. He went right to the register box and came back with the notebook to where she stood at the picnic table.

"Here," he said, handing her the register. "Sign it."

"What's the hurry?" she said, taking it and laying it down on the picnic table. She was about to take off her pack, but he stopped her.

"We're not staying here."

"I'm tired," she whined. "I can't go any further."

He opened the book in front of her.

"Sign it," he said. "Do it. Now."

What was up with him? His tone was so cold and demanding.

She took the pen and for a brief moment she considered hurling it into the trees. But something wasn't right and she composed a short entry.

Saw a little deer, she wrote and signed it, *Spoiled Little Princess*.

Collin who had been standing behind her took the pen right out of her hand.

"Hey!" she said. "What's up with you?"

She stood glaring at him as he quickly wrote a few words. Just before he closed the notebook, she glanced down at his entry.

Saw a really huge bear. It's been following us for the last mile. He signed it, *Juvenile Delinquent*.

Her eyes grew large.

"Are you serious?" she asked him. But she already knew the answer.

He nodded.

"You know," she began. "I was feeling really tired, but I suddenly have a lot of energy to keep going."

There would only be another four miles to go to the next shelter. There was a solar shower there. Word on the trail was that you could even order pizza from the little town at the bottom of the north side of the mountain and they would deliver it up to the unpaved jeep road entrance to the shelter. Moving on seemed like a really good idea.

They returned to the Appalachian Trail from the blue-blazed side trail that led from the shelter. Brooke glanced back and saw the bear. She gasped and wanted to run.

But Collin grasped the back of her left arm before she could bolt and held it firmly.

"We are not running," he said quietly.

For the next two miles, Collin kept his hand on her arm. She didn't mind that he was forcing her to keep up with him. When they reached the Route 645 road crossing, they looked back. The bear had stopped pretty far back but it was still right in the middle of the trail. He released his hold on her arm.

"I think he's staying there," said Collin. "I think it's okay now."

Brooke stared at Collin. He didn't have to wait for her like he did back there and warn her about the bear. He could have just left her to face it alone. But he waited for her and then he kept himself between her and the bear.

Collin saw Brooke was rubbing her arm and noticed a red mark where his hand had been.

"Sorry," he said. "I tried to make some noise when I first saw it, but it wasn't scared. It didn't move out. When I saw it wasn't going to leave, I thought we should."

"How much farther must we go?" Brooke asked.

"Two more miles."

"At least this part isn't that rocky."

But within a mile the rocks began again and made the going slow.

"I had to open my mouth about the rocks, didn't I?" she said.

They could hear the traffic on Route 501 even before they reached an open pipeline and a panoramic view to their right. They heard another noise just above them and looked up.

Not fifty feet overhead was a hang glider floating in circles. The hang glider waved to them and descended into the valley below.

The white blazes cut back into the trees and they followed the trail to another even more scenic overlook and paused. They could see a city far to the southeast and lights beginning to twinkle on as the light slowly faded from the sky. They stared at distant mountains and the big valley below them.

"What city is that way over there to the left?" Collin asked her.

"I don't know," she said.

"But you're from Pennsylvania, aren't you?" he asked.

"Well, it might be Reading," she said. "Yeah. It's Reading. I was there once when I was campaigning with my father. They have a Pagoda on top of the mountain that overlooks the city. It's supposed to be the only Pagoda east of the Mississippi River." She pointed off into the distance. "See that red dot at the edge of that mountain. That's the Pagoda."

"That tiny little dot?" said Collin, squinting to see the faint red light on the distant mountain.

"Yep," she said.

"Do you know what?" he said to her.

"What?"

"Right here at this spot we have exactly one hundred miles to go."

"Really? That's a lot, but it's better than two hundred. Now, I just want to get into my sleeping bag. How far do we have to go?"

"The shelter is just on the other side of the road."

They left the view, crossed the road and in seconds were stowing their packs on bunks in the enclosed shelter. Brooke then turned back to the door and wrapped her arms around it and hugged it, whispering something that Collin couldn't hear. Later he read her short register entry.

Thank God for doors, she had written. *I feel so vulnerable out here, especially after I saw the hugest bear I ever saw. I hope I never see another one even half that size.*

Other hikers came straggling in to spend the night at the shelter. They too had seen the bear, but all they had on their minds was ordering pizza. There was a menu sitting on the table inside the shelter.

Brooke picked up the menu and looked at all the selections, then put it back down on the table. She had no money.

"Uh, J.D.," she began. "Do you have some money left?"

"Yeah, some."

"You know I don't have any money on me, but if you loan me just a little, I promise I will pay it back."

He totally doubted that she would.

"How ironic is that, Princess?"

"Beyond words, ironic, J.D., but you know where I live, right?"

"The first castle on the right when you head into Harrisburg. So if I knock on the drawbridge door just past the moat, the doorman will give me my money?"

"Yes," she said, trying not to roll her eyes and trying hard not to sound perturbed by his jesting comments. "You'll get your money."

He shrugged and passed her the menu.

They found what they wanted and borrowing a cellphone they called their order in.

Collin and Brooke waited with the other hikers along the road for their food to be delivered. When the car pulled up, Collin didn't head back to the shelter to eat it.

"Where are you going?" Brooke asked him.

"I want to eat it at the overlook," he said.

"Sweet," said one of the other hikers. "I'm going too."

Soon six hikers were eating pizza at the Kimmel Lookout.

A young couple who had parked their car over at the roadside parking lot walked down to the lookout.

"Is this like a local hangout?" one of the hikers asked the couple.

"Yeah," said the guy. "It's probably the shortest piece on the entire Appalachian Trail in Pennsylvania where you can access such a great view."

"Tons of people come here," said the girl. "Families, dudes on motorcycles, old people, young people, everybody. A lot of people also hike over to Round Head. There's an overlook there, too. That's three miles heading north on the trail, but it has to be one of the rockiest sections in Pennsylvania. There's also lots of rattlesnakes in those boulders. You can hear them down in the rocks."

"There's another lookout with an awesome view that a lot of hikers miss," the guy told them. "Just before you get to the lookout at Round Head there's a little campsite off on your left. To the right there's a tiny trail. It looks more like an animal trail than a side trail. Turn there. On a clear day, you can't believe how far you can see. When you look to the north you can see over the saddle of the ridge you were just on. You can see Route 81 so far to the north the tractor trailers look like ants. If you look to the southwest, you can see the Cumberland Valley, you know, that long flat farmland section you were on a few days back. You can see the mountains on both sides of that great valley. It's a dead-on match to the elevation profile on your trail map. It's very cool. But the really best view is some thirty miles further north on the trail at the Pinnacle. Well, technically it's actually a few yards off the Appalachian Trail. But when you're at the Pinnacle, you can look north and see where you will be hiking in the next few days. Over at the lookout near Round Head, you can look some seventy-five trail miles back and see where you were."

"We'll have to check that out," said one of the hikers.

As the stars came out the hikers lingered, lying on their backs looking up. A bright shooting star crossed directly over them high in the sky.

"Awesome," someone said.

"Wow," Collin heard Brooke whisper.

A small hint of a smile crossed Collin's face. Up until today, he didn't think that it was possible that Brooke would have even noticed the shooting star much less be impressed by it. It was about time she started enjoying something out here.

After a while, the hikers gathered up their empty soda bottles and pizza boxes and headed back to the shelter.

While on the Appalachian Trail in Pennsylvania, northbound hikers can look just ahead of them and see Round Head where they will soon be.

Chapter 16

It was a rocky start as soon as they got on the trail the next morning. Rocks were everywhere, but mostly they were right in the middle of the trail.

Brooke could not have imagined every different kind of rock there was. Some jutted straight up, some were on their sides. Some were sharp, others more round, but all were a pain to have to walk over.

They stopped at one overlook and could see the distinctive shape of Round Head at the end of the curve of the mountain to the right up ahead of them. They could see a few open rocky areas along the ridge top.

"One of those open areas must be the lookout that that couple was talking about," Collin said to Brooke.

As they crossed a small boulder outcropping they heard a sound they had not heard before.

"What's that noise?" Brooke asked.

Collin looked down into the crevices between the boulders and saw movement.

"It's rattlesnakes," he said, surprised at how many there seemed to be slithering around on the ground below them. "If you stay on top of the boulders and keep moving, it will be okay."

"I hear them everywhere," she said. "I swear when I get through with this, I will never go near anything like this ever again."

They made their way quickly past the boulders and were back to the ordinary run-of-the-mill small rocks strewn along the trail. In less than an hour they found the campsite on their left that the couple mentioned. On the right they saw the small trail.

"I'll wait here," said Brooke.

Collin walked through the trees to the rocky opening on the edge of the mountain. He looked to the north, over the saddle of the mountain where they had just been. He could see tractor-trailers far to the north, as small dots glinting white in the morning sun traveling along the interstate and disappearing into the distance. To the west was mountain ridge after mountain ridge. And far to the southwest he saw the mountains drop away to the great valley. He sank against a boulder and just stared. The sweeping green valley just below him looked enchanting and so peaceful, like a picture. The large side of the mountain they had just come across looked so magnificent and immense. He let the sun warm him and he took off his pack. He could not rush away from this place.

After twenty minutes he heard Brooke calling.

"Where are you?"

"There's no snakes over here, Princess," he yelled. "C'mon over."

Reluctantly she made her way over to him.

"Check it out," he said to her. "See that long flat section way in the distance. That's that big stretch of farmland we walked in the Cumberland Valley. You can see Center Point Knob from here. This is awesome. We walked this whole entire piece of Pennsylvania, Princess. As far as the eye can see. We hiked all this country."

Brooke studied the amount of land they had covered, then looked up at the proud little look on Collin's face as he stared off into the distance.

She found herself smiling. He looked happy.

He glanced over at Brooke and smiled at her.

"This is awesome," he said. "There's just no other word to describe it."

Suddenly they realized they were smiling at each other and they quickly stopped and looked away.

"Well, I guess we should get going," he said, reaching for his pack.

In another three miles they came to a dam near a place called the Hertlein Campsite. The water was so cold they couldn't bring themselves to swim in it. They did not linger there but continued on.

Less than four miles later they heard traffic before they could see it. Up on a tree they saw a little sign that said *Route 183*.

They cleared the trees and came to the road and stopped.

"This is it," said Collin quietly. "This is where it happened."

Collin stood there and watched as the cars came speeding around the curve from the south side of the mountain and they were only going the speed limit.

"I don't remember getting hit," he told her. "I didn't even know what happened until I saw it on TV. And they kept showing it again and again."

He looked over at Brooke.

"You hurt me," he said.

"I didn't do it on purpose. You ran out in front of me."

"You were speeding and you took off. You didn't care."

"I already said I was sorry," she said, sounding cold and indifferent. "Besides, you're okay now."

There was nothing nice or warm about her, Collin thought. There was no compassion or kindness in her.

With a lull in the traffic, they crossed the road.

Collin touched the Appalachian Trail sign.

"To Maine," said Brooke reading what it said.

No, they were not going to Maine, Collin thought.

"No," he said aloud. "To New Jersey."

They entered the trees and they crossed more rocks, lots of rocks.

"They should hire somebody to get rid of these rocks," Brooke whined. "This is ridiculous. Why can't they make it easy? Maybe it wouldn't be so bad if they cleared the path. If it was clear you could do it on rollerblades or do it on a bicycle and you could finish it that much quicker. You know, you can't even look around or you'll trip. You always gotta be looking down, watching where you put your feet."

"I'm sorry, did you say something?" Collin said, pretending he didn't hear her complaining.

"You heard what I said."

They walked in silence over the rocks, until Collin spoke up.

"So, do you want to check out the Eagle's Nest Trail that leads to the lookout?"

"Not really. Where is that?"

He pointed to a sign directly over her head.

"See," she said. "That's what I'm saying. I can't ever look up unless I stop, because I always have to be looking down watching the trail."

"But the lookout is historic," he said. "I thought you said a senator's daughter was all about history."

"Not this kind of history, but what's so historic about this place in the middle of nowhere?"

"The Eagle's Nest lookout was where one of the Appalachian Trail maintaining clubs was founded back in 1916. Some guys came hiking up the south side of the mountain to look for an eagle's nest they heard was up here. Some say they found the nest, but there was no eagle in it. But they did find a pretty spectacular view at the top and they had so much fun hiking up the mountainside together that they wanted to do that hike again and again and they decided to form a hiking club. Ten years after they founded their club, they began working on constructing the Appalachian Trail and they built the 102 miles of the trail from the Susquehanna River to the Lehigh River."

"That's a nice history lesson, J.D.," she said sarcastically, "but I don't want to check out the view if it's not right on the trail."

"Fine," he said and they walked on.

A short time later he spoke up again.

"I'm going to fill up my water bottle."

"Where?" she asked.

He pointed to a sign over her head. It said *Sand Spring Trail*.

"The spring is just down the hill," he told her.

They left the white-blazed Appalachian Trail and took the blue-blazed side trail down to the spring. After filling their bottles they returned to the trail and continued on for another half mile.

"Wait, don't tell me," said Brooke. "I see it."

"What?"

"The sign for the Eagle's Nest Shelter."

They turned left onto the side trail to the shelter.

"Where is it?" Brooke asked after they walked a while. "It should have been here by now."

"According to the guidebook, it's like a total of three tenths of a mile off the trail. It does seem long."

They finally arrived at the wooden shelter and they took off their packs.

"Check out this little shelf," said Brooke, as she set up her little stove on the sill along the outside wall of the shelter. She mixed rice and dried vegetables from a pouch into her boiling water. "Do you know what I am hungry for? French fries."

"Hot deep fried chicken fingers," he said.

"Potato chips," she added.

"And real cold lemonade."

"A big glass of frosty cold chocolate milk followed by a large chocolate milkshake."

"And a hamburger," he said.

"And a large Caesar salad and a hot turkey sandwich, with French fries and gravy."

Collin set up his stove and threw his pasta noodles with powdered alfredo sauce into his boiling water.

"A cold apple," she said.

"And a hot piece of apple pie," he added.

"How far are we from the next town?"

"Eight miles," he said.

"How much money do you got on you?"

"Twelve dollars."

"All I have is a worthless piece of gold colored plastic. If only I had my phone. Oh, I'm so angry! And I'm so hungry!"

As they stood there mixing their food they heard some hikers approaching. Down the trail came some hikers they hadn't seen since they first started.

"J.D. and the Princess," the hikers called out.

"Rock Man and Southern Cross," Collin called out to them. "I thought you would have been way up ahead of us. What are you doing behind us?"

"We took a couple zero days in Duncannon," said Rock Man.

"It was more than just a couple zero days," said Southern Cross. "Rock Man found a bull's-eye rash on his leg. The doctor told him he has Lyme disease."

"But I'm still here," said Rock Man. "I see you two are also still here."

"Yeah," said Collin. "We have less than one hundred miles to go. Can't let anything stop us now."

Southern Cross built a fire in the fire ring before he set up his little trail stove to cook his macaroni and cheese.

"I understand there's a place in Port Clinton that has some good food," said Southern Cross. "I hear if you order a small plate of French fries it's like a little mountain and if you order the large order, it's a mountain huge enough for three people to eat."

"That's what I want," said Brooke.

"French fries and a good cold beer," said Southern Cross.

"French fries and a good cold ice tea," said Rock Man. "I'm on antibiotics."

"As long as they have French fries," said Brooke, "that's all I want."

When they signed the register that night, Collin and Brooke both mentioned food.

Tonight all we can think about is food, Collin wrote. *Something tasty and good.*

One of the first things I'm going to do once I am out of here is look for a restaurant that has a buffet menu and then I am going to spend the day there, Brooke wrote.

The sky was full of clouds as the sun went down and as dawn broke the following morning it was totally overcast.

The four hikers left the shelter together and stayed together making their way over the rocks. When they reached the Auburn Overlook, they gave it a quick glance and kept going.

As they approached the break in the mountain at the Schuylkill Water Gap, they began a steep one thousand foot drop down into the tiny town of Port Clinton.

"I do hope," Brooke began, "that the climb up tomorrow will not be like this."

"I hope not, too," said Collin, "but I'm sure it will be."

They took their time going down the mountain. Loose rocks slid under their feet and made them lose their footing. Leaves lingering from last fall made the trail slippery and made them keep their eyes focused on the ground continuously.

When they finally reached the bottom, they crossed over railroad tracks and then a bridge that took them over the Schuylkill River.

"Hey," said Brooke. "This is the same river that goes past the Philadelphia Art Museum. I was there a bunch of times. Who knew it came all the way up here?" She caught herself and added, "But it's not like I really care."

They made a right turn and crossed a second bridge over the Little Schuylkill River. And as they entered town, there sat Brooke's friend in her car.

"Laura," Brooke gasped. "How did you know I was going to be here? I'm so happy to see you."

She wrapped her arms around her friend.

"Girl," said Laura, "Look at you! Look how great your legs look! C'mon, I got us a room at the bed and breakfast and I'm taking you out to eat."

"How did you know I was here?"

"This is the third day I came here and sat watching for you. Every time I saw another hiker come down off the mountain I asked them if they saw a girl hiker named Brooke. Nobody even heard of you. They asked for your description and when I told them what kind of pack you had, they called you a horrible name."

"Yes," said Brooke, rolling her eyes. "I'm the Spoiled Little Princess."

"That's awful. They kept insisting that was your name and I told them they were wrong. But they said you were with the Juvenile Delinquent. Well of course I knew right away they were talking about *him*."

Laura and Brooke looked over at Collin who was standing just inches away from them with the two hikers.

"Hey, Princess," Collin said. "Your friend is really rude."

"She wasn't talking to you," Brooke said.

"She's talking about me," Collin shot back, "and I'm standing right here."

"Anyway, Brooke," Laura continued. "All the hikers I talked to kept saying you were still behind them somewhere, so I knew it was only a matter of time till you got here. So I just decided to wait, and here you are. Now, come on, Brooke, let's get out of here."

Brooke looked at Collin.

"See you," he said to her. "I'll be at the Hiker Hostel Gazebo in the Park, just down the road. I'll be leaving at first light."

With Southern Cross and Rock Man, Collin walked the half-mile down the road to the open air Hiker Hostel. It was a gazebo in the middle of the park, a free place for hikers to stay overnight. The only drawback was all the noise from the cars and trucks rolling down the roadway just above them.

"Let's check out that place with the French fries," said Rock Man.

Rock Man, Southern Cross and the Juvenile Delinquent walked down the middle of the small town street until they found it.

"Here it is. The Little Bear Pub," said Rock Man. "Oh, I get it. Instead of a little bear cub, they call it the Little Bear Pub."

They found a booth in the restaurant and they each ordered a plate of large French fries.

"And I'll take a large cheesesteak sandwich, too," said Southern Cross.

"Me, too," said Rock Man.

"Make that three," said Southern Cross pointing to Collin.

"No," said Collin. "I can't. I don't have enough money."

"It's on me," said Southern Cross. "I know what's going on with you having to walk with that girl."

"It's not that bad," Collin said.

"Yeah, right," he said. "Everybody out here on the trail knows what's going on. What do you want to drink? Soda? Ice tea? Whiskey?"

"Ice tea," he said smiling. "Thanks."

By the time their French fries came, they saw Laura and Brooke walk in and take a booth across the room.

"Oh, they're here, too," said Laura. "You can't even get away from him for a meal. Do you want to sit on this side so you don't have to look at him?"

"No, that's okay," said Brooke. "This side is fine."

Collin saw Brooke come in. She looked all clean and was wearing a new set of clothes. She was also wearing make up for the first time since she started the trail. Even though she had a new outfit, he noticed she was still wearing her hiking boots.

"So what's he like?" Laura asked.

"He's all right, well, some of the time."

"Is he mean and weird?"

"I thought he was going to be, but he's been kind of nice. He's been keeping an eye out for me. He tries to act like he's not, but he has been."

"What do you mean?"

"Well, there was this huge bear on the trail and it kept following us. He took my arm and he made me walk fast so I wouldn't get behind him. He was protecting me. And before that we were in this bar and it was getting rowdy. He didn't tell me to leave. He just said that he was going up to the room, like he didn't want to leave me alone there. I don't know if it was because of the other hikers or the townies that were there, but everybody was pretty tanked-up."

"Well I guess he's never seen you at some of those insane parties in Washington."

Brooke smiled.

"Yeah, we had some wild times. That's a whole other world. It's different out here. I can't see any of those guys in Washington ever doing this or caring like he did when we saw that bear."

"You like him, don't you?" said Laura.

"Of course not," Brooke said quickly.

"I think you do."

"Maybe like an annoying little brother."

"No," said Laura. "He might be a year younger than you, but I wouldn't say he was the brotherly type."

"No?"

"No," said Laura. "He's got this tough, but sensitive thing going. And, you know what? He's not ugly like I thought when I first saw him. He's actually kind of cute."

"No, he's not."

"Yeah," said Laura. "He is."

Laura saw Brooke glance over at Collin.

"Sorry, girl," Laura said. "But it's all over your face. You do like him."

"Don't even joke like that, Laura. I hate him because I wouldn't be here if it wasn't for him. Why didn't he look before he walked out into the road? He would have got hit anyway by someone else. Yesterday I saw that road where it happened. Any of those cars coming around that curve at the speed limit could have hit him. It wasn't my fault."

"Yeah, Brooke, maybe it was his fault that he walked out into the road, but you were speeding and you took off. If you would have stopped…if you would have been going a little slower…if you would have just stayed there, you wouldn't have to be out here doing this."

"I'll be glad when this is done."

"Me, too, Brooke. So what do you talk about all day with him?"

"Nothing much. He's always trying to tell me things about the trail like I care, but I don't care."

"What do you do all day?"

"Just walk. Search for water and purify it. Cook supper on these strange little things they call stoves. Think about food. Find the shelters. Sleep on the hard floors. Sleep on hard bunks. It's just really awful. But it's weird, like I feel like I'm kind of getting used to it."

Throughout the meal, Collin would glance over at Brooke and then Brooke would glance over at Collin.

Once their eyes met. Collin nodded to Brooke and Brooke nodded back.

"I can't wait until you are done with this ridiculous travesty," said Laura. "Social media and all the entertainment shows are saying it's all a political ploy by your dad to show he can get control of his out of control daughter."

"No," said Brooke. "That's not true. But Collin said the same thing, like he knows something I don't."

"Who knows? The media could be wrong. They are also saying you are not really out here hiking the trail, but you are."

"Laura, you need to get me a phone," said Brooke.

"I'm sure there's someplace near here where we could buy one."

"No, not now. When I see you further north of here. But let me borrow your smartphone for a second."

"If you're looking for info on the trail, Brooke, I already downloaded an Appalachian Trail GPS app if that's what you need."

"Yes, that's exactly what I need. Let's see… some place north of Port Clinton but before the Delaware Water Gap. Okay, there's the Lehigh Gap. There's the Route 248 trail crossing. There's the town of Palmerton. Okay, let's make it Palmerton, like in three days. And I need some money. Maybe about $500.00."

"Anything else?"

"Yeah, but I'll let you know next time I see you in the town of Palmerton."

All night long, the hikers staying in the gazebo listened to the sounds of traffic from the highway and rain on the roof. In the middle of the night they heard a noise even louder than the tractor-trailers: thunder.

Brooke awoke in the night and listened to the rain and the thunder, wondering briefly how the guys were doing out in the gazebo in the storm. She was glad she didn't have to be out there.

The next morning in the pouring rain Collin said good-bye to Rock Man and Southern Cross at the trailhead while he waited for Brooke. She didn't come.

After a while, Collin decided to see if Laura's car was at the bed and breakfast so he walked over to it. The car was not there. Brooke was gone.

He went back to the trailhead. He thought for sure she would be there. She wasn't.

Looking back one last time, he left the town of Port Clinton. He followed the Appalachian Trail along the river, then under the highway bridge and began the climb up out of the Schuylkill Water Gap.

Many times he glanced back wondering if he would see her. He kept a slow pace since the rocks were slippery.

It was only six miles to the Windsor Furnace Shelter. Beyond that was the climb up the mountain to Pulpit Rock and the Pinnacle.

He hoped he didn't leave without her, that maybe she was still back in town, but he had waited for her and she hadn't showed.

"It's on you, Princess, to catch up to me," he said aloud.

Even though it was raining, the woods seemed so peaceful. The tree trunks appeared so much blacker when they were wet. The leaves, so much greener.

He went on slowly, but frequently looked back and listened to see if she was calling for him as she had done before.

After he had gone a couple miles, he realized she was gone and wasn't coming back. Why should she? She hated it out here. She complained about everything. She didn't like being dirty and not being able to take a bath every day. She was scared of the bears and the snakes.

"Yeah, I guess if I were you, I wouldn't want to come back either," he said to himself.

He was on his own now walking through the trees and stepping over the rocks without having to contend with her. It was nice, but it didn't feel right.

Reaching the top of the mountain, he made fast time on the uneven ridge. There were a few minor ups and downs and one long downhill. The rain stopped just as he crossed a small bridge over a little creek that was now running fast from all the rain. He went past a sign that said open campfires were forbidden in this area and around the bend in the trail he saw a blue-blazed side trail to his left that led to the Windsor Furnace Shelter.

He paused a moment wondering if he should even bother going over to the shelter to sign in. It seemed pointless to hit every shelter and sign in if the Princess was no longer with him.

He checked his map. He had only gone six miles that day. It was too early to stop hiking.

The next shelter was not for another nine miles, yet between the Windsor Furnace Shelter and the Eckville Shelter there were two mountaintop overlooks, Pulpit Rock and the Pinnacle, that he wanted to see the view from on a clear day. And from what he had heard back in Port Clinton, the weather report for tomorrow was going to be a picture-perfect glorious June day, the only kind of day to be up at a mountaintop overlook like the Pinnacle.

He decided to take the blue-blazed trail to the shelter.

"Hey, slacker," Brooke yelled out to him. "Where have you been? Where were you?"

"Where was I?" he asked her, surprised to see she was already there. "What are you doing here? Where were you?"

"We drove to the gazebo but some hiker said you had already left. So I went to the trailhead and you were gone."

"I was at the trailhead waiting for you and I left to see if you were still at the bed and breakfast, but the car was gone."

"And you thought I got off the trail? Quit? With seventy miles left to go?"

"Well, yeah," he said. "And here you were ahead of me the whole time. I kept looking back."

She handed him the register.

"Sign it," she said.

He opened it to add his entry and saw what she wrote.

The Spoiled Little Princess is no quitter, he read.

He wrote a short entry, too: *And neither is the Juvenile Delinquent.*

Chapter 17

In the middle of the night, Brooke was awakened by a voice.

"... and it's two miles to Pulpit Rock," she heard Collin say.

"What's going on?" Brooke asked him. "Who are you talking to?"

"You."

"I didn't hear what you were saying. Say it again."

"I was trying to tell you that it's two miles up to Pulpit Rock."

"Are you talking in your sleep?" Brooke asked him. "Or are you awake?"

She heard him come over to her side.

"I'm awake. I want to hike up to Pulpit Rock and watch the dawn come."

"No," Brooke groaned. "It's the middle of the night. Go back to sleep and leave me alone."

"No," said Collin. "If we leave right now and don't dawdle, we can watch the sun come up."

"Collin, I'm too tired. Go ahead if you want."

"Okay, I'll wait for you up at the Pulpit," he said and was gone, off into the darkness.

Brooke lingered a moment and knew she did not want to be there all alone in the dark.

"Darn you, Collin," she said, rolling out of her sleeping bag and reaching for her boots. She put on her little headlight, quickly packed up her things and was just a few minutes behind Collin in reaching Pulpit Rock.

They sat there in the dark for half an hour before the first faint light came over the mountains on the horizon to the east. The sky was a deep violet but as dawn came, deep shades of red cascaded across the entire eastern sky, while the valley below was still in darkness.

It *was* beautiful, Brooke thought staring upwards. She looked over at Collin to tell him so, but she hesitated and watched him as he continued watching the sky. There was a look of pure contentment on his face, a look so peaceful that she didn't want him to lose it.

Sure it was a pretty sunrise, but it was just a sunrise, it wasn't like getting a new car or new jewelry or clothes.

"Man, I could stay here forever," he said.

"Hey, it's nice and all that," she said speaking up, "but there will be another sunrise tomorrow and the day after that."

The look of peace faded from his face and was overcome with a look of melancholy and she regretted opening her mouth.

She didn't understand, he thought as he stared at her. She was always taking things for granted and minimizing the truly good things in life.

"This sunrise we saw today, we will never see again," he said. "You can't duplicate it. You can't buy something that beautiful for all the money in the world."

He picked up his pack and walked slowly along the trail. They crossed over big boulders and a thousand little rocks over the next two-mile stretch to the Pinnacle.

Collin crossed over the last of the boulders until he reached the rocky overlook known as the Pinnacle and stared out at the panoramic view in front of him.

Below him was a large valley made of fields and farms and homes and hills and far to the left was the long, long ridge of the Blue Mountain.

"This is awesome," he said, slowly removing his pack and sitting down on a wide rock ledge.

"That's for sure," said a voice directly behind him. "I think that same thought every time I come here."

Collin turned and saw a man wearing a small day pack.

"Are you from around here?" Collin asked him.

"Yeah, about twenty miles up the road. I hiked up here in the dark from Eckville just to watch the sunrise."

"We saw it from Pulpit Rock."

"Good times," said the man. "Where are you hiking from?"

"We came from the Maryland border and we're heading to the Delaware Water Gap on the Appalachian Trail."

"Yeah? In that case I have to point this out to you. See that ridge, way off to the left?"

"Yes," said Collin.

"The Appalachian Trail follows that whole ridge. Those cell towers are where Route 309 crosses the trail. That little bump way over yonder is Bake Oven Knob. Past that is the dead zone of Lehigh Gap. That's where the zinc smelter killed all the vegetation on the mountainside. That area was a Superfund clean-up site, but there's been a lot of steps taken to regenerate the foliage in that area, so it's looking a lot better than it was."

Collin reached for his map and studied it.

"Lehigh Gap, that's 30 trail miles away," said Collin. "And the Delaware Water Gap is another 36 miles after that."

"Yeah, but that's not the Delaware Water Gap where it drops off there at the end."

"It's not?"

"No," said the man. "Here, look on your map. See just past Wind Gap. Check the contour lines past Pen Argyl and just north of Roseto. That's what you are seeing."

"Wow, that's pretty cool. I'm glad you were here to tell me that."

"Where are you from?" the man asked.

"Nebraska. We have nothing like this out there."

"It's good you got to see this view on this beautiful day. You should stay here as long as you can, but I have to be moving on. Enjoy your hike."

"Thanks," said Collin.

Collin sat at the overlook looking over every house and barn and rise in the land.

"Hey Princess, it's only five miles to the next shelter. How about if we spend the day here?"

When she didn't answer him he glanced over to where she was sitting. She had fallen asleep against a nearby boulder with her backpack on.

"I'll take that as a yes," said Collin.

Sometime around noon while Collin was snacking on raisins and nuts, Brooke woke up.

"How long was I sleeping?" she asked him.

"A long time."

"Why didn't you wake me up?"

"You looked like you needed the sleep. And I needed to sit here and look at the view."

She yawned and stretched.

“How far is the next shelter?” she asked.

“Just over five miles. They have a solar shower there.”

“And the one after that?”

“The Allentown Shelter is another seven or eight miles.”

“Any big hills?”

“Yeah, there’s about a thousand foot climb right after the Eckville Shelter.”

She reached for a protein bar and some chocolate covered nuts and took a drink of water.

“What do you want to do?” he asked her.

“Hit the Eckville Shelter and keep going to the Allentown Shelter.”

“Okay,” he said.

The trail after leaving the Pinnacle was a wide grassy level pathway with fewer rocks than they had seen for a while. They reached an open field in the middle of the mountain.

“What’s this?” she asked.

“They land helicopters here if a hiker is injured.”

The trail veered to the right and it descended down into a narrow valley. When they reached the road they turned right and followed the road to the shelter.

“It looks like a little shed,” said Brooke. “I’m going to take a shower and then we can keep going.”

“Okay,” said Collin. “I’ll sign the register awhile.”

He brought the notebook from out of the shelter and sat down at the picnic table to write his entry.

The view at the Pinnacle was awesome. The hike down was easy. The miles are flying by. I want it to last as long as possible while the Princess seems like she is going into overdrive to do some major miles in order to reach the end. And then what? What will happen when we get there? He signed it, *Juvenile Delinquent*.

Brooke quickly finished her shower and came over to sign in her brief entry.

"*Great solar shower! The Spoiled Little Princess.*"

"I'm taking a shower, too," he said.

When he was done, he sat at the picnic table to put his boots back on just as another hiker came in off the road.

"Can we order pizza here?" the hiker asked Collin and Brooke.

"I don't think so," said Collin. "There's not really any town around here. It looks like the next pizza stop isn't for another 25 miles in Palmerton."

"Palmerton?" Brooke said. "Let me see that map." She wanted to see the elevation profile. "So we have a big climb and then mostly ridge walking and then like a two mile long descent."

"And I heard there were a few thousand rocks and some serious boulders up in that section," said the hiker. "Are you staying here tonight or are you heading to the next shelter?"

"We're aiming for the Allentown Shelter," Collin told him.

"Maybe I'll see you in Palmerton," he said.

Collin and Brooke made their way back up the road, entered the trees and began their climb up the mountain.

"This just keeps going and going," said Brooke. "When are we going to get to the top?"

The trail curved around and Collin saw a sign.

"Hawk Mountain is two miles this way," he said. "Want to check it out?"

"Are you crazy? That's two miles over and two miles back. Four extra miles just to see another mountain? I don't think so. What's so special about Hawk Mountain anyway?"

"It's the world's first sanctuary for birds of prey."

"Boring," she said. "Besides, I don't want to get into the shelter after dark."

"That's not boring. It's a place where people can watch hawks and eagles migrating. That's a very cool thing."

They continued walking and reached Dan's Pulpit and took a short break.

"We're at the top," said Collin.

"Good."

"Look," said Collin pointing to the Pinnacle across the valley. "That's where we were yesterday."

They continued on, past Balanced Rocks and reached the Tri-County Corner, where the Pennsylvania counties of Berks, Lehigh and Schuylkill converged.

"Check it out," he called to Brooke. "It's history." He pointed to a little sign and read it aloud. "Tri County Corner. Construction of the Appalachian Trail in Pennsylvania started here on November 21, 1926."

"Boring," she said.

"Did you ever think of all the people who work to keep this trail open?" Collin asked her.

"No," she said. "Never."

"It's all done by volunteers. Volunteers built it. Volunteers maintain it."

"I can think of a thousand other things to volunteer to do."

"I think it would be fun to hike on into the trail and trim back branches and cut out blow-downs," said Collin.

"I think you're crazy. They couldn't even pay me to do that."

They came to another sign to their right that told them that at this point one trail maintaining club's territory ended and another one began.

A short time later they arrived at the Allentown Shelter and Brooke sat down immediately.

"I'm beat," she said. "And I'm hungry for pizza. Ever since that guy mentioned it, I've been thinking about it all day."

"Yeah, me too," said another thru-hiker who came up just behind them. "And tomorrow that's what I'm having for supper."

"Where are you getting pizza?" Brooke asked him.

"Palmerton," he said. "It's only 17 miles ahead. We could be there by mid-afternoon."

"Why can't they have restaurants and real hotels right on the trail?" Brooke asked. "This is ridiculous."

"That's the Spoiled Little Princess you're talking to," said Collin.

"And you must be the Juvenile Delinquent. I heard about you both. Nice to meet you. I'm Wandering Will from Wisconsin." He looked down at her feet. "Where's the high heels?"

"Very funny," said Brooke, tired and not in the mood for hiker humor.

Brooke boiled water and threw in noodles with chicken flavored seasoning. Just as soon as she finished eating and had cleaned her pan, she fell asleep while Collin stayed up to talk to the hiker.

"So Wandering Will from Wisconsin, how did you get your name?" Collin asked him.

"I like to wander. I also like to wonder. Sometimes I sign the trail registers Wondering

Wandering Will, but mostly I sign them Wandering Will. I like to check things out, like back there a few miles, I saw that sign for Hawk Mountain and I had to check it out. They had some nice lookouts and they had a visitor's center. It was pretty cool. I think I already hiked two thousand miles, just by exploring a lot of side trails."

"That's what I want to do," said Collin.

"Well, maybe next time around you can."

The next morning Brooke had already finished breakfast and was ready to go while Collin was just stirring from his sleeping bag.

"I'll catch up, if you want to head out," Collin told her, seeing how impatient she was to get going.

"Okay, bye," she said quickly.

As fast as Brooke was that day, Collin was the direct opposite. He couldn't bring himself to get under way. Wandering Will was taking his time, too, finding in Collin a kindred spirit who did not want to race to the end of the hike just to get the trail completed.

"You miss a lot when you're in a hurry," said Wandering Will. "I don't understand why some people want to see how fast you can hike from Georgia to Maine. Like why don't you just get on a treadmill in a narrow hallway and paint the walls green, because that's all you'll see if you go fast. Everything will be one green blur."

"And the views," said Collin. "How can you hurry past an incredible view?"

"You can't," Wandering Will agreed.

They crossed Route 309 and then the Knife Edge, a short but narrow boulder outcrop that dropped steeply on both sides. When they passed by Bear

Rocks, they both scrambled to the top of the boulders to look at the view.

As they reached the next road crossing they caught up to Brooke.

"Look at all this trash," Collin lamented, staring at beer bottles and empty snack bags strewn in the large parking lot.

A pickup truck pulled up and the driver jumped out and waved to Collin, Brooke and Wandering Will.

"Did you have a party here?" Wandering Will asked him.

"Not me," he said, pulling out some empty trash bags. "I'm the trail maintainer for this section. Local kids like to party here and I try to get here as frequently as I can. But sometimes I just can't keep up with the trash. Perhaps when you finish your hike you all could get involved with maintaining the trail."

"Yeah, that's not likely," sneered Brooke.

"That wouldn't be the Spoiled Little Princess, would it?" said the man. "I heard all about you." He looked at Collin and Wandering Will. "And that makes one of you the Juvenile Delinquent."

"That would be me," said Collin.

"I got candy bars and some cold sodas," he said, opening a cooler in the back of his truck.

"Awesome," said Wandering Will.

"Yeah, thanks," said Collin.

The trail maintainer wished them luck on their journey and the three hikers continued on their way.

The trail was smooth for only a short time, when the rocks began again. There was a short rocky uphill climb to two overlooks. To the left they could see mountains to the north; to the right they could see the valley to the south.

Wandering Will and Collin checked out the views on both sides while Brooke continued on the trail.

The next half mile was a challenging section of boulders that slowed their pace. They stopped at the Bake Oven Knob shelter just to sign the register and to eat a quick lunch.

Brooke's entry was short and to the point: *These rocks really suck. The Spoiled Little Princess.*

Collin's was a little longer: *Saw some awesome views today. This section of the trail has been challenging with all the boulders. Found out that littering is not limited to the cities, but it is up here, too. We have 44 more miles to go to the Delaware Water Gap. I want to go as slow as possible, but the Princess is in a hurry.*

They crossed Ashfield Road and after a long walk uphill in the trees they came to a fork in the trail.

"I guess this is where we part company," said Wandering Will. "I'm going to take the North Trail."

"You're getting off the Appalachian Trail?" asked Collin surprised.

"Just for a couple miles. I'm not a true trail purist."

"A purist?" said Brooke. "What's that?"

"Someone who doesn't miss an inch of the trail," Wandering Will explained. "The North Trail parallels the Appalachian Trail for a couple miles and then meets up with it at the gap. The North Trail has a long continuous view the whole way and I want to see that."

"I'd like to see that, too," said Collin, "but we have to sign in at the Outerbridge Shelter."

A big smile spread over Wandering Will's face.

"You won't miss the shelter at all. The North Trail meets back up with the Appalachian Trail before the shelter."

"How does the judge even know if we are signing in at all the trail registers, anyway?" Brooke asked. "Tell me, J.D., how would he know?"

"He'll know," said Collin. "Your father probably has spies out all over the place to keep an eye on me."

"You mean the judge?"

"The judge, your dad, your mom, all of them."

"Yeah, right. And aren't we supposed to stay on the Appalachian Trail?"

"Like you always do what you're supposed to do?" Collin asked her.

"Well, you're the one that loves the Appalachian Trail so much," she said.

"The judge only said we had to walk the length of the Appalachian Trail and that's what we'll be doing."

For a long moment they stared at each other.

"I don't care which way we go as long as we get to the end," Brooke said finally.

"Okay, then let's go," said Collin folding his map.

Chapter 18

From the moment they passed a radio tower and came out on the north side of the mountain, a sweeping panoramic view lay before them.

They could see the far ridge of the mountains to the north running parallel to their mountain. Up ahead on the left in the distance they could see the town of Palmerton down in the valley below.

As they followed the trail, a well-worn path in the mountaintop grass, they could see part of the highway below as it came towards the mountain they were standing on.

They watched as cars came from out of the distance, and made their way like ants along the highway. The cars disappeared into the tunnel at the base of the mountain a thousand feet below them.

"That's the northeast extension of the Pennsylvania Turnpike," said Collin.

No clouds were in the sky. The sun was beating down on them, but a cool air from the north made it feel comfortable to walk.

"It doesn't get any better than this," Collin said aloud.

Brooke rolled her eyes.

"You don't like this at all, do you?" Wandering Will asked her.

"No," she said.

"What do you like to do?"

"I like to go to parties. Hang out with friends. Go shopping."

"I guess you go to a lot of parties," said Collin.

"Constantly. Last month I was in California twice and New York a half a dozen times for parties."

"I wonder what that's like," Collin said aloud.

"What?" she asked him.

"Going to parties."

"What? You haven't been to one for a while?" she asked.

"I've never been to any."

"What are you talking about?" she said. "Everybody goes to parties."

"No, not everybody."

At first she thought he was joking, but then she realized he was serious. For a long time she stared at him.

"How is that even possible?" she asked in disbelief.

"Not everybody is lucky like you are," Collin said.

"Then," she said suddenly. "You can come to Washington next January when my father is elected president. There will be so many parties and you can come to them all."

"Yeah, like that's going to happen."

"My father is going to be the president," she stated fiercely.

"I don't mean that," said Collin. "I'm sure he will be president. But think about it. What are the chances of me ever hearing from you after the Delaware Water Gap? I know you, Princess. I know there is not even the tiniest remotest chance of a possibility of that happening."

And it wasn't like he would ever want to see her again, he thought to himself as he walked on ahead of her.

"Yeah," said Brooke calling up to him. "You're right. What was I thinking?"

The three hikers walked on in silence until they reached the promontory point on the western side of the Lehigh Gap.

"Look at that mountain," said Brooke. Her mouth dropped open as she stared at the looming east face of the Lehigh Gap across the river. It was the biggest mountain she had seen on the trail so far. "Don't even tell me we have to climb that."

"What's the big deal?" said Collin. "How is that side different from this side?"

"It looks huge," she gasped.

"It kind of reminds me of the Eiger," said Wandering Will. "It has that same kind of concave look."

"What's the Eiger?" Collin asked.

"A mountain I saw over in Switzerland, only this is a tiny little mole hill compared to that."

They continued down the mountain and linked back up with the Appalachian Trail. When they reached the Outerbridge Shelter, they paused just long enough to sign in.

Less than forty miles to go. Spoiled Little Princess.

Brooke passed the notebook to Collin.

It was a good hike today. The weather was perfect. Loved the blue sky. I'm really looking forward to the climb out of the gap tomorrow. Juvenile Delinquent.

They descended into the gap and stuck out their thumbs for a ride into town. A pickup truck stopped in a couple minutes and the three hikers jumped into the back.

They crossed the bridge over the Lehigh River and were soon in the small town of Palmerton.

"Do you know where the hostel for hikers is?" Wandering Will asked the driver.

"I think it used to be in the jail, but I think they moved the cells and now it's just the big basement in the municipal building. Either way I think you're supposed to check in with the local police in order to stay there."

"Is that the only place we can stay?" Collin asked.

"Yeah, I think it is. They don't let you sleep in the town park."

The thought of staying in a jail, even if it was no longer a jail, did not appeal to Collin. When he stopped by to look at it, he saw it was just a big, old, open room with lots of bunks and shower facilities. Maybe it wouldn't be so bad, he thought.

They registered with the police department, first Wandering Will, then Collin. They waited outside for Brooke to finish.

"She seems to be taking a long time," said Wandering Will.

Collin went back inside to see what the hold up was, but he met Brooke coming out the door.

"What?" Brooke asked.

"Nothing," he said.

They returned to the municipal building and each took a shower. Collin pulled out something to eat from his dwindling food supply.

"No," said Wandering Will. "Put that away. The pizza is on me. Let's go and find it."

The three hikers walked through the town in search of the first pizza place they could find and went in. It seemed the restaurant was used to feeding hungry hikers, for the food came quickly and they ate it just as fast.

"You said your father's running for president," Wandering Will began. "Obviously he could have prevented you from having to do this."

"That's what Collin said a while back," said Brooke. "But the judge… He's the one that sentenced us to do this…"

"Yeah, right," said Wandering Will.

"You think this was a scheme they were all in on?" Brooke asked.

"I'm just saying that if you think about it... Out of control daughter… future president can't control her… He needs a novel way to show the country he can deal with her. If he's an effective father, he'll be an effective president. He makes a deal with the judge and everyone's happy."

"No," said Collin. "Everyone's not happy. Why punish me, by making me do it with her?"

"You were the pawn they needed to make it legit," said Wandering Will. "Anything to further her father's chances."

Collin glared at the girl. It's what he had known all along.

"It's just how it is," Brooke said, quietly. "Can't you just let it go? So my father was using me, too. It's all just part of the game."

"No, it's not a game," said Collin. "This is my life and you were all just using me. Everyone was… your dad, the judge, all the lawyers... You used the right word, Will. A pawn. That's all I am to these people, a pawn, the lowliest, most inconsequential, useless piece on a chess board."

"No," said Brooke.

"Yes, Princess. And do you know what was worse than being exploited by your people? It was you and how you acted the entire time from that moment back on that road when you hit me to the way you looked at me in that courtroom and every day out here… like I was nothing. Every time you opened your mouth out here… I don't know how you could have been any meaner to me."

"No," she said again, but Collin stopped her.

"Yes," he said, his voice sounding more agitated. "I know some guys who did some really bad things… some of them are going to be locked up for a very long time… the others… they walk around with guns and knives and would not hesitate one second to use them… but do you know what? I would rather be with them than you. With them, a person knows what they're up against, unlike with you and your kind… with your mean, conniving and deceitful ways."

"I'm not conniving or deceitful," Brooke said. "And I'm not mean."

"Why couldn't you have just tried to be nice?"

Collin got up and left the restaurant.

Brooke sat there, angry and upset.

"It's just how it is," said Brooke. "I can't help it."

"I guess it all depends on if you want to live in the White House or not?" said Wandering Will. "Either way, you still go back to your life and Collin goes back to his."

"I don't care about Collin. He means nothing to me."

"I know that and he knows that. That's what he was just telling you. But you've spent a lot of time hiking with him. When this is over you might not miss him, but you'll think about him often and what you both went through out here."

"I will not," said Brooke.

She walked out and went back to the building where they had planned to stay. Collin wasn't there and neither were his things. She went back outside to look for him and Laura pulled up.

Boulders on the Appalachian Trail in Pennsylvania, between the Bake Oven Knob Shelter and the Bake Oven Knob overlooks.

Chapter 19

"Laura," she said, hugging her friend.

"I got here as fast as I could."

"You got everything?"

"Yes."

"You have to give me a ride," said Brooke.

"Why? What's the rush?"

"Collin left. I think he's getting back on the trail and I gotta catch up with him. I just have to grab my pack."

In seconds, she was hopping into her friend's car.

"Let's go."

Laura drove her back across the bridge, to the road where they had hitched a ride earlier that day. Brooke watched the road for any sign of Collin.

"He's not here. Let's go check out the other parking lot."

They drove back across the Lehigh River and as they entered the long parking lot at the base of the mountain on the eastern side of the gap, Brooke caught sight of him.

"There he is," she said. "Hurry."

"I can't hurry. There's lots of potholes here."

"Just go," said Brooke.

They reached the edge of the parking lot at the base of the mountain and Brooke jumped out. Grabbing her pack she pulled it on and left with a quick good-bye to her friend.

Already, she could see Collin pulling ahead of her high up the trail. As she stared up at the large mountain looming over them, she started to shake. She was not a mountain climber and that mountain in front of her looked terrifyingly steep and incredibly high.

"Collin," she yelled. "Stop."

Whether he didn't hear her or he didn't want to stop, he kept going. And she did too.

The trail got steeper and steeper with a few switchbacks. Breathing hard and with her heart pounding inside her chest, she struggled to follow the white blazes and keep him in sight.

"Stop, Collin," she called out, but her voice was lost in the wind.

The mountainous trail soon became boulders and the walk soon became a climb. This was not a section to be doing in the dusk. Glancing down, she was frightened at how high she was, but she had gone too far to stop now. Then she reached one small section where she had to use both her hands and feet to pull herself up and she froze, unable to go up or down.

Further up the face of the mountain Collin felt free. He greatly enjoyed the scramble up the boulders, but most of all he was happy because he was done with the Princess.

The wind subsided and he heard a noise that sounded like a kitten.

"What is a cat doing up here?" he thought.

He continued, but stopped when he heard it again and looked down. There below at that one strenuous piece, he saw Brooke.

"Why is she even bothering with this charade?" he said aloud. He paused and shook his head. Then finally, he pulled off his pack and headed back down.

Brooke was crying, her face pressed against the rock wall, unable to move up or down. He watched her several seconds before he called down to her.

"Well," he said, sitting down inches above her. "If it isn't the Spoiled Little Princess. What are you crying for, Princess?"

"Shut up," she screamed at him. "Quit making fun of me."

Her pale face held a look of pure terror.

"Come up and make me."

"I can't move."

"Awww, maybe you need your Daddy to call in the National Guard for a rescue," he said, his voice full of ridicule.

"Stop it," she cried.

"You are so pathetic. There you are stuck on that one tiny piece of boulder, like it's the hardest thing in the world. Poor stupid little princess."

"I hate you," she screamed at him.

"And I hate you, too. Isn't that nice that we feel the same way about each other? Well, I have to be going now. Have fun standing there all alone in the dark."

"No, wait, you have to help me."

"I don't have to do anything, especially for you."

"Don't leave me here."

"Good-bye, Princess. I would say see you later, but I won't be seeing you later or ever again."

"No, don't go. You can't leave me here."

"Oh, yes I can," he said, laughing loudly at her.

"Stop being so mean to me," she cried.

"How does it feel, Princess? How does it feel? I learned good from you, didn't I?"

"I'm going to kill you," she screamed at him.

"You have to reach me first. Besides, you tried that once. You weren't very good at it. Good-bye, Princess."

He left her and climbed out of sight.

Adrenalin from fear and anger rushed through her. With her hands reaching as high as she could and pushing with one leg at a time, she inched her way up that one little section of the rock wall and got past the steepest and hardest part of the Appalachian Trail in Pennsylvania.

Trembling with fear she turned her head and found herself face to face with Collin.

He was right there. He had not left her.

"I hate you," she said crying.

"I hate you, too," he said.

But he immediately put his arms around her, and gave her a tight hug and flashed her a gentle smile.

"You did it," he whispered. "It's okay."

He released her and took her hand.

"C'mon, now. It's dark and we gotta get going."

Emotionally and physically exhausted, she did not let go of his hand until they got past the boulders.

Night descended and they were miles away from the next shelter. They placed their sleeping bags under the signpost for the Winter Trail at the top of the mountain and fell fast asleep. Neither the sound of the wind nor a distant pack of coyotes disturbed them that night.

They ate their breakfast of bagels in silence the next morning before continuing on. They walked along the top of the mountain, where few trees grew.

As they passed under some power lines, Collin took off his pack and followed the lines off to the right.

"I'll be right back," he said. "I have to check out the view."

He made his way through the long grass and scrambled up the boulders at the base of the power line support towers. He was hoping for a view to the south but he was surprised to see a 360-degree view.

From where he stood, Collin could see the mountain range they were standing on running eastward a distance before it veered to the north. Checking his trail map he saw that the Appalachian Trail ran east along the Kittatinny Ridge before veering to the north toward the Delaware Water Gap and New Jersey.

"Awesome," Brooke could hear Collin say. She looked over to where he was and saw him standing on the topmost boulder studying whatever he was looking at in the distance.

In a few minutes he was back.

"You should have seen it," he said. "A complete 360-degree view. And way up ahead you can see the whole ridge we are standing on as it veers to the north."

He put on his pack and they continued onward.

"Just over thirty miles to go till New Jersey," Collin said to her as they crossed Little Gap Road and continued onward to Smith Gap.

"How many miles to the next shelter?"

"Just under eleven."

"So that would mean there would be like twenty miles left after that."

"Yes," he said.

"This could be our last night on the trail," said Brooke. "Couldn't it?"

"It could. But there is an incredibly rocky section after Wind Gap. That could make the going real slow."

"But it's possible?"

"Yeah," he said. "It's possible."

They turned off at the blue-blazed side trail and spent the night at the Leroy Smith Shelter.

I hope this will be the last night out here, Brooke wrote in the register. *It will be like a marathon tomorrow, but I want to be out of here.*

Early the next morning they came off the mountain and crossed the road. A steady wind blew on them and they knew they were in Wind Gap. Its name lived up to its reputation.

"Okay, so we did over four miles," Collin said to her as they crossed Route 33. "It's nine miles to the next shelter, or sixteen miles to the Delaware Water Gap. If we keep going we could get those sixteen miles done and finish it today."

"Any big mountains?" she asked.

"Here, look," he said showing her the map. "We have this climb out of Wind Gap, but it's all a ridge top walk until the descent at the end which looks pretty steep. And then we have the walk over the Delaware River."

"We can do it," she said.

"Well, we'll aim for the Kirkridge Shelter and see how late it is till we get there."

They climbed out of the gap and began one of the rockiest sections they encountered on the whole Appalachian Trail in Pennsylvania. They couldn't take their eyes off the trail for one second without stopping or else they would trip over the rocks.

Pointed, jagged and strewn continuously right along the middle of the trail, the rocks made the walking difficult and the pace exceedingly slow.

More than three hours and nine miles later, they crossed the road at Fox Gap.

"That was the worst section on the whole trail," said Brooke.

"That was the most rocks I have ever seen," Collin agreed.

In a few short moments they arrived at the Kirkridge Shelter and signed in.

"*Seven miles to go till New Jersey*," wrote Collin. "*We're almost there. No one knows we will be finishing the trail today. If they did, I wonder who would be waiting there to pick up the Spoiled Little Princess, her folks or just her limo driver. I know who would be waiting for me: the caseworker waiting to lock me up into a nether world of existence. Collin Talley, aka the Juvenile Delinquent.*"

He handed the notebook to her so Brooke could make her entry. She read what he wrote first.

"My folks are out in California campaigning," she said to him. "There's no way they'll be coming. Besides, they never expected us to get done this fast. It will just be the camera crews."

"What camera crews?" he asked. "How would anybody know we're going to finish it today?"

She shrugged without responding to him and picked up the pen and began to write.

"*This has been hell. I do not like camping out. I can't wait to take a bath and sleep in my own bed again. I will be free of the Juvenile Delinquent and he will be free of me forever.*"

She stood up and picked up her pack.

"I want to keep going," she said. "I don't want to spend one more night out here."

"Okay," he said, picking up his pack. "Let's do it."

They walked to Tott's Gap and onward to Mt. Minsi where Collin stopped and looked down at the Delaware River.

"There it is," he yelled to Brooke as he stared at the river from atop the mountain. "The Delaware River is in sight. We're almost there."

"Good," said Brooke, but as usual, she did not care about the view.

They angled away from the south side of the mountain and stopped on the rocks on the eastern most edge to look at the view of Mt. Tammany on the New Jersey side of the Delaware Water Gap.

"Thank God, I don't have to go up that," gasped Brooke.

"Man, I can't wait to go up that," Collin stated. He looked over at Brooke. "We came 230 miles."

"It seemed like two thousand."

"What did you like most?"

"We didn't get there yet," she answered.

"What did you hate most?" he asked.

"Getting on the trail."

He was silent a moment then began to speak.

"The thing I hated most was having to do it with you," he said. "But then after a couple days out, I was glad to have someone to hike with." He stared down at the river below and continued. "The things I liked most, besides the other hikers, were the views. That first one in Pen Mar was nice. I liked the view from Hawk Rock where the Juniata flowed into the Susquehanna, and I liked the view from the Pinnacle. I really liked the climb up out of Lehigh Gap. And I liked that view from the lookout just before Round Head."

He looked up at the sky as the sun sat low on the western horizon.

"Look at those colors. The deep blue, the reds, the orange. It's so beautiful it almost hurts," he said, his voice almost a whisper. "I wish I could stay here forever." He was quiet again. "I can't wait to do the whole thing from Georgia to Maine. I want to sit on McAfee Knob and I want to see Max Patch and Roan Mountain and the Green Mountains of Vermont and the Whites of New Hampshire and I want to stand on Katahdin. I hope they let me do it. I'll die if they lock me up in some prison until I'm eighteen."

"Why would they lock you up?"

"You don't understand," he said. "I'm only fifteen. They won't let me be on my own."

"You don't have any family anywhere?" she asked him.

"No."

"So, where will they make you go?"

"I hope at least to a foster home. Living with a bunch of people I never saw before would be better than juvie. But that is only if they catch me. And they're not going to. By the time we get over into New Jersey it will be late and dark and nobody will even be around. C'mon, we'll be in New Jersey soon and you can go back to your life and be happy again."

They could hear traffic from the interstate, even though they were still at the top of the mountain. They began their final descent, heading down into the gap on the north side of the ridge by following the switchbacks.

"Doesn't this seem like it's taking forever and ever?" Brooke asked.

"Yeah, because it's late and we're doing a twenty mile day."

There was one final view at Lookout Rock that Collin needed to stop at.

"I'll be right along," he said to Brooke.

She knew he would catch up to her quickly. The steep downhills slowed her down as much as the steep uphills.

Long before she reached the boulders over Eureka Creek, he caught up to her.

"I'm going to have an ice cream milkshake as soon as I get out of here," said Brooke.

"A thick chocolate milkshake sounds good."

"With cherries," she said.

"No cherries on mine."

"It got dark fast," said Brooke in the waning light.

"Because we're deep in the gap on the sunrise side of the hill."

They came out of the woods, passed by a little pond on their left and reached a parking lot. Brooke stopped.

"Is this New Jersey?" she asked Collin.

"No," he said. "We're not in New Jersey until we cross the river."

They hung a right at the end of the driveway and followed the white blazes into the town of Delaware Water Gap. The white blazes continued onward out of Pennsylvania and into New Jersey.

"We did it," Collin said to Brooke as they walked across the Interstate 80 Bridge over the Delaware River. "We covered 230 miles of trail in eighteen days. Can you believe that? That's like an average of thirteen miles a day. You did a lot better than I thought. At the beginning I figured it would take us three months to get across Pennsylvania. You did good, Princess."

"I'm glad it's done."

They reached the New Jersey side of the river. Their journey together was done.

As they approached the parking lot they could see it was overflowing with cars.

"I wonder what's going on," Collin said to Brooke, seeing a massive array of lights ahead of them.

"It's for us," she said. "Those are reporters and camera crews."

He stopped.

"*You* contacted them?" he said.

"Yeah, I had to."

"No," he cried. "I didn't want it to be like this. Don't you understand what this means?"

"There's not really that many cameras," she said. "Really, this is nothing. You should see it when my father has a press conference or when he's out on the campaign trail. He usually has a whole entourage following him in a bus. It's been like this ever since he announced he was running for president."

She would never understand. She was focused on the cameras, while he was focused on his life and the fear that he would now be stopped for sure.

But then he looked at all the people. Perhaps he would be able to disappear into the crowd and keep going.

"Well, Brooke," Collin said quickly. "I wish I could say it's been fun hiking with you, but it wasn't."

"Hey, you called me Brooke. I didn't think you knew my name."

"Yeah, but Spoiled Little Princess just seemed to fit you better."

“There they are,” someone in the crowd yelled and the reporters swarmed Collin and Brooke.

Collin and Brooke took off their packs as a dozen cameras recorded them.

“Miss Setree, can you tell us of your experience?”

Collin turned to look at Brooke wondering what kind of comment she would make to them. Despite her tired appearance Brooke looked poised and confident.

“It was wonderful,” said Brooke. “I’ve learned a lot about myself, about Collin and, more than I could have ever learned in any text book about the many places of scenic beauty that we have throughout the great state of Pennsylvania.”

Collin glanced at her, his mouth opened in surprise. Leaning closer to her, he whispered in her ear.

“What a load of crap,” he said quietly.

“Thank you, Collin, that was so sweet,” she said, smiling and speaking loud enough to be heard on the microphones. She leaned over and kissed Collin on his cheek. Looking back to the cameras she continued talking. “I’d like to thank the judge who sentenced us to this journey together. And I look forward to seeing my parents.”

“What are your future plans?” a reporter asked her.

“Well, I’ll be changing trails. I will be leaving the Appalachian Trail to go on the campaign trail with my parents. Although I can’t say for sure which one is more strenuous.”

She paused until the laughter subsided.

“Then after that, I plan on spending the next eight years in the White House with my parents and after my good friend here, Collin, finishes the whole

Appalachian Trail, he will be coming to live with us at the White House."

There was a loud murmur from all those present.

"And your folks know about this?"

"Collin is like a little brother to me, even if he is taller than me." She put her arm around him. "And I always wanted a little brother. And as you know, my mother and father always got me what I wanted. Thank you all for being here."

Brooke ended the media conference there and then. Taking Collin's arm, she pushed their way through the crowd.

"That was an Oscar award winning performance," Collin said to her.

"Thank you," she said. "I thought you'd like it. I think they ate it up, too."

"It's all so fake."

"I want to go to the White House," she said. "And I will do anything and everything possible to see that that happens." She was silent a moment. "Oh, by the way, sorry about the kiss. I just got into the act. Let them all wonder what happened."

"You mean what didn't happen," said Collin.

"Yeah, whatever. Thanks for not saying anything."

They saw her limo sitting in the parking lot.

"Well, there's my ride," Brooke said, heading toward it. "Take care of yourself, Collin."

And that was it, Collin thought. He was free of her.

The camera crews and the crowds dispersed and the parking lot emptied, as the limo driver opened the door for Brooke.

"Westin, I am so happy to see you," she said.

"You look exhausted, Miss Setree."

"Only because I am."

She glanced across the lot and saw a car pull up in front of Collin and a man, perhaps a caseworker, got out. The man approached Collin. She watched as Collin slowly kept backing away from him.

Brooke and her driver watched as the caseworker moved closer and closer to Collin.

"But I did what the judge ordered," they heard Collin say. "I'm free now. You can't touch me."

"Collin," said the man. "Let's talk about this in the car."

"No, I did my sentence. You can't lock me up."

"Collin, you are only fifteen. Get in the car."

"No," said Collin.

Finally the man stopped him. Brooke watched in amazement as the man shoved Collin against the car, placed Collin's hands behind his back and handcuffed him.

"It didn't have to be like this," the caseworker said to Collin. "You could have made it easy on yourself, but with your track record for running it's better this way, anyway."

"It's just like he said," Brooke said aloud.

"What's that, Miss Setree?" the driver asked her.

"I'm going back to my castle and he's going back to his dungeon. We have to do something."

The chauffeur drove up quickly to the caseworker's car and jumped out.

The caseworker was ready to force Collin into the back seat of the car when he glanced up and saw Westin standing there.

"What are you doing?" Westin asked him. "Why are you putting your hands on him? Why is he in handcuffs?"

"I am taking him into custody and I'm not taking any chances. Now why don't you and the young lady get back in your car. This is none of your business."

"You're not taking him," Brooke yelled, closing the back door before the caseworker could put Collin inside the car. "I won't let this happen. You can't lock him up. He's old enough to take care of himself."

"We can't have this, young lady," said the caseworker. "We can't have this." He looked at Westin. "Would you please ask Ms. Setree to get in her car?"

"No," said Westin. "Perhaps you need to get into *your* car. But first, I think you had better let the young man go."

The caseworker paused.

Dressed in his custom-made black suit, the limo driver looked more like a high-priced lawyer than a chauffeur.

"Do you have a warrant for his arrest?" Westin asked.

"No," said the caseworker. "I don't need one."

"Why, yes, as a matter of fact you do," said Westin. "See, you have no jurisdiction here. We are in New Jersey. And you are from Pennsylvania. Unless you have a warrant, you cannot take him. Now remove the handcuffs and take your hands off him or you will be sued for false imprisonment and charged with kidnapping across state lines, which as you know is a federal offense."

"And you are?"

"I am Westin Prescott of Mercer, Woodbine, and Butler, and Mr. Talley is in my custody."

The caseworker hesitated a moment and then reluctantly removed the handcuffs from Collin, got in his car and took off.

Collin sank against the limo and caught his breath.

"Oh, man, that was close," said Collin, wiping the sweat from his forehead. He looked up at Westin. "Are you a lawyer?"

"No, just the limo driver."

"But how did you know what to say?" Collin asked him.

"Oh, that was on a cop show I saw last night."

"You'll probably get in trouble with them for impersonating a lawyer," Collin said. "I know how they are."

"I never said I was a lawyer," said the driver. "Mercer, Woodbine, and Butler is not a law firm. Those are the towns back in western Pennsylvania that I lived in when I was a kid."

"Thanks," he said to the driver.

Collin looked over at Brooke. She actually did something nice. "Thanks, Princess," he said.

"Look, J.D., maybe I don't hate you so much any more, but don't go thinking that I like you or anything."

"No, Princess, I would never think that."

"I just figure that I owed you for saving me at Lehigh Gap and for that big old bear."

"Are you ready to head out now, Miss Setree?" the driver asked Brooke.

She was. But as she watched Collin reach for his backpack, she saw his hands were shaking from his close call.

He had shown himself to be tough and strong and brave on their whole trail journey, but at that moment she realized he was just a scared kid all alone in the world. She could not just leave him like that.

"No," Brooke said shaking her head. "I'm going to stay here tonight."

Collin glanced over at her in disbelief. Why wouldn't she want to get out of here as fast as possible, he wondered.

"Collin," she said. "How about we rent a couple of rooms in town? I'll go home tomorrow."

"I don't have enough money left."

"Look, I'm the Spoiled Little Princess, aren't I?"

"Yeah."

"I've got to live up to my reputation, don't I? After all what good is having money if I can't spend it. We're taking a zero day tomorrow so we can get some supplies. For you, not me. I have no intention of doing another inch on the trail. Look, Collin, it's too late for you to start at Springer in Georgia if you want to get to Katahdin before the snow comes. But you could make it a flip-flop. Keep going north to Maine and then come back to Pen Mar and hike south to Springer. Besides, there are some pretty cool hikers heading north right now that you could be hiking with."

"Yeah, there are."

"Head north and when you get to Maine call me. I'll get you back to Pen Mar Park and you can hike south to Georgia. A flip-flop is better than no thru-hike at all, don't you think, J.D.?"

"Yeah, Princess. A flip-flop would work."

Brooke motioned Collin to get into the limo.

"Look," Brooke continued. "You'll need more food and some more fuel for the stove. But we'll talk about that tomorrow. Let's get cleaned up and go eat."

The following afternoon Collin was standing in New Jersey, his pack full of new provisions. In his pocket was a wad of cash and a smartphone, presents from the Princess.

"I guess this is it," she said, saying good-bye to Collin. "Have fun. Text, instant message or call me. Let me know if you need anything, except someone to hike with. That I can't help you with."

"I don't know what to say," said Collin.

"Say, 'I'll send you a selfie from Katahdin, Spoiled Little Princess'."

A smile crossed Collin's face.

"I can do that," he said to her.

"And when you are finished, I really meant that about coming to the White House in January."

"No, you didn't. That was for the cameras. I get how the game is played. You all do it very well."

"I didn't mean it at first, but look at this text from my Dad."

Brooke, not sure about legal proceedings for adoption of a child in foster care, but we have the best lawyers working on it. Looking forward to seeing you soon. Love, Dad.

"Look, Collin, this is only if it's what *you* want. There's no games, no angles or any pretentious displays for popularity polls. It's just that I want you to know that if you need a home port when you're done wandering, you have a place with us. Anybody who can put up with me for 230 miles can deal with the rest of my family, with anything."

"I'll think about it. But I could never live like you do. I couldn't. I just want a little log cabin in a forest somewhere… I never really fit in anywhere before."

"You're okay, Collin. You fit in fine with the hikers. They all loved you. And you know what? The Spoiled Little Princess likes you, too. She does. And you'll fit in just fine wherever you go, but I hope you will come to Washington, even just to visit."

"Maybe I could do that."

Brooke threw her arms around Collin.

"Good luck, Collin. You be careful out there. Watch out for bears."

"Bye, Princess," he said.

He headed north on the Appalachian Trail. She watched him make his way up the hill until he was nearly out of sight.

Collin was happy. He was on his way, feeling alive and free and strong. He reached into his pocket for the smartphone from Brooke. He would put it into his pack next time he stopped, for he already had one in his pocket… the one the judge had given him back in Pen Mar Park, that only he and the judge knew about… the one the judge had sworn him to secrecy to carry without telling Brooke… the one that he was told to use to take pictures of each shelter they were to stop at, so the judge would know they were signing each trail register… the one the judge gave him in case hiking with Brooke was more than he could bear... the one the judge gave to him because the deputy from Kepner Creek had put in a good word for him, which shocked Collin beyond words when the judge told him that.

"No," said Collin, shaking his head. "That deputy wouldn't do that."

"Yes," the judge insisted to him. "And do you know what the last thing he said to me was?"

"Probably something like why don't you toss him in jail and throw away the key?"

"No. He said I should be kind to you."

"No," said Collin. "No, he wouldn't say that..."

"But he did. And he said you were a good kid and I know you are. You complete this sentence, Collin, and you can hike wherever you want when you're done. And I have one thing to say to you: don't put up with any of Brooke's crap. She's not any better than you are, even though she thinks she is. Out on the trail you are equals. Give back to her whatever she gives to you."

Collin came so close to using the phone when Brooke maced him, but he resolved not to jeopardize his chance to be free. He came close to blowing it all when he took off after leaving the emergency room.

He had never trusted authority and he had his doubts that the judge would actually keep his promise to him. When the caseworker showed up at the end, Collin thought for sure the judge had lied to him.

But the judge sent him a quick text first thing that morning.

It was a processing error. Your file was still open with Youth Services. Jeff was just doing his job. Westin is a pretty sharp guy. Your file in PA is now closed. But don't be a stranger. Call me and let me know how it's going.

Collin was thinking about everything that happened on their trail journey as he turned back and waved to Brooke one last time before he disappeared around the curve in the trail.

Brooke smiled and waved back.

"He's gone," Brooke said to her driver. "Let's go home."

"Think he will make it?" Westin asked her.

"Yes. He'll make it."

She rolled down the window as the car crossed back into Pennsylvania and she stared up at the deep blue sky and let the wind blow her hair.

Today she would be with her friends. Tonight she would be back in her own bedroom. There would be no more shelters, no more filtering her drinking water. She would have a bathroom with hot running water for a long hot, soapy, bubble bath.

As they headed in opposite directions, Brooke pulled out her smartphone and opened the Appalachian Trail GPS app, checking for the next road crossing north of the Delaware Water Gap and how far it was to the next shelter.

Collin and Brooke's Hiking Log:

Day	Miles Hiked	Where We Stayed
1	5	Deer Lick Run Shelter
2	10	Rocky Mountain Shelter
3	13	Birch Run Shelter
4	6	Toms Run Shelter
5	11.1	Tagg Run Shelter
6	11.7	Boiling Springs Campsite
7	15	Darlington Shelter
8	10.9	Duncannon
9	11.7	Peters Mountain Shelter
10	18	Rausch Gap Shelter
11	17.5	Route 501 Shelter
12	15	Eagle's Nest Shelter
13	8.5	Port Clinton
14	6	Windsor Furnace Shelter
15	16.4	Allentown Shelter
16	18.8	Atop Lehigh Gap
17	14.5	Leroy Smith Shelter
18	20.5	Delaware Water Gap
	Total : 229.6	

66994210R00131

Made in the USA
Lexington, KY
29 August 2017